RESOURCE CENTRE
Skate School

The world's coolest boarding school!

A beautiful scene unfolded before Frankie's eyes, skaters gliding hither and thither over the glittering ice. She so wanted to join everyone. Her heart pounding with nerves and excitement, she moved forward, gently stepping onto the ice. She gripped the barrier, paused for a second and took a deep, steadying breath as majestic thoughts filled her mind.

She was no longer a hobby skater.

She was part of Team GB.

This was where her Olympic dream began.

Filled with a happy confidence, Frankie pushed away from the edge, stroking her blades over the ice. Left…right…

WHAM!

Endorsed by the
National Ice Skating Association, UK

"Every budding ice skater will love this book."
Liz Littler, NISA International
Championship Judge

Skate School

Ice Princess

KAY WOODWARD

USBORNE

For Anya, with love

First published in the UK in 2009 by Usborne Publishing Ltd., Usborne House, 83-85 Saffron Hill, London EC1N 8RT, England. www.usborne.com

Cover photograph © Graham Taylor. Skater: Stephanie Rigley.

The name Usborne and the devices ♀ ⊕ are Trade Marks of Usborne Publishing Ltd.

A CIP catalogue record for this book is available from the British Library.

FMAMJJASOND/10   96181   ISBN 9780746099254

Printed in Yeovil, Somerset, UK.

Chapter *One*

Frankie Wills just couldn't resist. Slowly, she reached out of bed and patted the velvety darkness until she found what she was looking for – her trusty holdall. She pulled back the zip, smiling as the metallic growl clattered noisily. Then she tucked her hand inside, running her fingertips over the cracked leather and the cold metal blades. Frankie sighed happily. Her precious ice-skating boots. She *never* tired of them – just a single touch was enough to whisk her away into a dreamy world where everything was calm, silky-smooth and totally magical—

Beep-beep-beep!

Quickly, she silenced the alarm with a deft karate chop and sprang out of bed. It was 5.30 a.m. Time to get ready.

As usual, she and Dad – after eight years, it felt just about okay to call him that – left the house at 6.30 a.m., far too early for conversation as far as either of them was concerned. London was just waking up, night-shift workers still on their way home, traffic jams still to come.

They walked through semi-deserted streets towards the bus station, where they hopped on board the slightly musty 48. Dad settled himself into the driver's seat and wriggled around until he was comfortable, before clicking shut the door of his cocoon and grasping the huge steering wheel with both hands. He'd been a bus driver since long before he married Frankie's mum. That's how they'd met. Mum had sprayed a purseful of change across the bus floor, while attempting to keep control of two squabbling children – Frankie and her brother Josh. Years later, after stubbornly avoiding promotion – why would he want to push a pen when he could drive a red double-decker? – Dad was still a bus driver. And despite the perspex barrier that now separated him from the passengers, he loved it.

Every day but Sunday, Frankie went with him. Not because she was an anorak-wearing bus-spotter, but because Dad dropped her off on his way, making the tiniest of detours to Lee Valley Ice Rink. Dad's bosses turned a blind eye – to them, she was little Frankie Wills, a sweet girl who wouldn't dare to stick chewing gum under the seats or backchat the driver. Except she'd been riding the 48 for so long now that she was no longer a sweet little girl. She was a fourteen-year-old ice princess.

Well, that's what she liked to dream.

This morning began like any other morning. By 7.15 a.m., she was at the rink, her blades carving graceful curves on the brand-new ice. The place was pretty much empty, apart from the caretaker and the odd early-bird skater. She didn't notice anyone else. But that wasn't surprising. Once she was skating, Frankie wouldn't notice if her entire family dressed in kilts and danced the Highland fling. Everything outside the barrier became a meaningless blur.

Then, at 8.15 a.m., it was on to school. Lessons next. Maths. English lit. It had all the hallmarks of a Normal Day.

It was at 4 p.m. that everything turned upside down.

Frankie arrived home to find the house silent. That was strange in itself. Usually, the noise would hit her like a giant fist – wailing in stereo from her twin baby sisters, accompanied by deafening rap music from upstairs.

"Is that you, Francesca?" said Mum. "We're through here, darling."

Frankie was really puzzled now. *Darling?* Yes. *Francesca?* No, no, no. She was never called that, not unless she'd spilled nail varnish on the dressing table or turned a white wash pink. She thought quickly. No, her conscience was just about clear. *So what was going on?*

Pausing only to kick off her shoes by the front

door, she hurried through to the kitchen. Mum and Dad were sitting at the table, each one balancing a twin baby girl on their lap. All four of them were staring goggle-eyed at the visitor.

"Er…hi," mumbled Frankie, when it became clear that no one had noticed her standing in the doorway.

"Darling!" said Mum, a toothpaste smile lighting up her face. "This is…" She paused. "I'm so sorry. How did you pronounce your name?"

The visitor nodded understandingly, as if she was used to having this amnesiac effect on people. "Madame Kristiana von Berne," she replied, getting to her feet. She extended perfectly manicured fingers towards Frankie, who fleetingly wondered why the name von Berne was so familiar, before grasping and shaking, wishing desperately that she'd wiped her own very sweaty hand on her skirt first.

The handshake was cool and firm, just like the visitor. Madame Kristiana von Berne smiled briefly, the movement causing barely a ripple on her perfectly made-up face. She was too striking to be beautiful, with dark eyebrows arching over icy-blue irises and scarlet, pouty lips that revealed film-star teeth. Her expensive outfit – tweed suit and skyscraper heels – would not have looked out of place on a Parisian catwalk. And she was *tiny*. Frankie, who was neither tall nor short, felt like a giant beside her. Quickly, she sat down and the visitor did the same, facing her across the scratched, wooden table.

"Madame von Berne watched you skate this morning," said Dad, beaming with pride. "She's an ice skater too. She thought you were good."

"I thought she skated well," corrected Madame von Berne. "For a beginner," she added, turning to Frankie. "How long have you been training?"

"Training?" repeated Frankie. She wasn't sure that messing about on the ice counted as *training*. Didn't you have to have a coach for that? "I've been skating for seven years," she replied, feeling incredibly nervous all of a sudden. "I don't really know what I'm doing. I just pick it up from the TV…" Her voice petered out. It sounded so *lame*.

"She never misses an episode of *Dancing on Ice*," Mum said helpfully. "That's where she picked up the…what was it called…? Triple Salchow scissor-flip!" she finished with a smile.

"And the double loophole," added Dad.

Frankie cringed. Her parents had a peculiar knack for inventing impossible new moves. It never bothered her usually. But they didn't usually have an actual ice skater in the kitchen – which reminded her… Why was this woman here? Had she made a special trip just to tell Frankie that she skated "well"?

Madame von Berne seemed to sense the unspoken questions. "I'm sorry to appear unannounced," she said to Frankie's parents with the awkward manner of someone who doesn't apologize very often. "It's not standard procedure at all. I'm afraid I tracked your daughter down via the ice rink – I hope you don't mind." She carefully smoothed her hair and turned to Frankie. "Let me introduce myself properly," she said. "I am Team GB's junior figure-skating coaching director, which means that it's my role to find and train future Olympic champions."

"Huh?" said Frankie, totally nonplussed.

"It's 'pardon', dear," said Mum. Then her jaw dropped. "*What?*"

Frankie just stared, goggle-eyed, as Madame von Berne's words ricocheted around her dumbstruck brain. *Figure-skating coaching director... Team GB... Olympic champions...* Was she dreaming? Were there hidden cameras recording her reaction? This was either the biggest send-up ever or...she was in serious danger of whooping so loudly she would burst eardrums.

The coaching director did not seem fazed by the stupefied response to her announcement. She calmly opened her brown leather briefcase and took out a small stack of business cards, handing one to Frankie. It was crisp, white and emblazoned with black, decorative lettering:

Madame Von Berne
Figure-skating coaching director
Team GB

"I think you have natural skating ability," repeated Madame von Berne. Her voice was cold and formal, without a hint of emotion. If she was joking, she was covering it up really well. "If your parents are in agreement, I'd be delighted if you would accompany me to Switzerland in order to develop that ability. We have a training school there – the skaters live on site. It's in the mountains in a rather idyllic spot. There, you will embark on a rigorous training programme, with a view to trying out for the Olympic team."

"Wow…" breathed Frankie. She was stunned, exhilarated…*terrified*.

"Wowowow!" copied her baby sister Meg, who had been quiet for far longer than usual. "Wow!"

"Waaaaaah!" howled Jess.

"Madame," Dad began, automatically reaching for a dummy and plugging it in. Jess sucked furiously. "The thing is…er, you see…I don't quite know how to put this…I'm not sure we can afford—"

"The training is, of course, fully funded," the coaching director interrupted calmly.

"Right-o," replied Dad, visibly relieved.

"Normal schooling is provided," continued the visitor. "Think of it as a boarding school with added ice." She smiled. Clearly this was a joke.

After a brief pause, everyone laughed.

Madame's face resumed its serious expression. "In return, we expect total commitment, absolute dedication and a huge amount of hard work. I can tell you right now, it won't be easy."

At last, Frankie found her voice. "W-when would I go?" she stammered.

"As soon as possible," replied Madame von Berne, leaning forward slightly. "We need to put you through some pretty intensive training before the British Junior Championships, to make sure that you're good enough to take part."

Frankie gulped. British Junior Championships? She watched them every year on the telly. Surely Madame von Berne didn't mean that she'd be competing in them…?

Apparently, Madame did. She reached into her briefcase once more. This time she pulled out a neatly stapled sheaf of paper. "Everything is explained here. If there are any further questions, do not hesitate to contact me." She closed the briefcase with an efficient snap and rose to her feet. "I do not expect a decision now. I shall give you three days to think about the offer" – at this, she looked directly at Frankie – "and then we will talk. Thank you so much for the cup of tea. I'd better be off."

Abruptly, in a blur of Parisian tweed, she was gone.

And Frankie's life had changed for ever.

Chapter *Two*

Frankie's first reaction to the imperious visitor's news had been to accept her tempting offer at once. But now she was having second thoughts. Was it what she really wanted?

It *was*, she told herself firmly. She'd dreamed of becoming a real figure skater for so long that the thought of living that dream every single day made her tremble with excitement. But it would mean leaving home, which made her feel horribly nervous too.

She didn't know *what* to think.

Mum and Dad weren't a great deal of help. One minute, they were hugging Frankie and saying how proud they were and how this was the opportunity of a lifetime; the next, that she was only fourteen, which was much too young to be leaving the country and that they'd miss her *so* much. If she didn't want to go, they said, that was absolutely fine. No, really, it was *fine*. And if she wanted to go, that was fine, too. That was the point at which Mum burst into tears. Frankie honestly didn't have a clue what they wanted her to do. Or not do.

The first thing her brother said was, "Can I have your bedroom?" And then, "When are you going?" But Josh grinned as he spoke and punched her half-heartedly, so she didn't think he really meant it.

The twins just babbled and were obviously no help whatsoever.

It was no good. Frankie was the only one who could decide. And to do that, she needed to get away. She needed peace and quiet – somewhere she could be alone, somewhere no one else could interrupt. Somewhere she could really *think*.

There was only one place to go.

The very next morning, thankfully a Saturday, Frankie set off with Dad again. Her destination: the ice rink. Was the journey shorter today? It seemed it. In no time, she was watching the 48 as it rumbled away from her. She was on her own. Swiftly, she walked into the familiar building and hurried to the changing rooms, where she unzipped her trusty holdall.

Her ice skates nestled inside. They were a birthday present. She could still remember the bubbling excitement she'd felt when she tore open the wrapping paper, not to mention the relief that she wouldn't have to wear those vaguely musty, horribly sweaty hire skates again. But, after the pounding Frankie had given them, her boots were well past their best. They were starting to pinch a little, too. Nonetheless, she couldn't bear to say goodbye to them. Not yet.

With clumsy fingers, Frankie pulled her laces tight. She clumped to the barrier, wondering if any ice skater ever managed to look graceful on dry land, removed the guards from her blades and…

Swoosh! She was gliding away from the edge and reality at the same time, entering a magical world of swirls and curves and loops and tucks, where movement was all that mattered. At the very centre of the rink, she raised her arms and began to spin round and round and round until everything else vanished. Her mind was whirling as fast as her feet.

Now she could think.

Should she go or should she stay?

Round and round...

It was what she had always wanted, wasn't it? Imagine being allowed to do what she loved best every single day... Bliss! She always watched the Winter Olympics and World Skating Championships with a mixture of awe and longing. It was an impossible dream. Now, she was one huge step closer to the dream coming true.

So why wasn't she jumping for joy?

Round and round...

The thought of leaving home was making her nervous, that was it. Even though her noisy, mildly dysfunctional family drove her crackers, she did love them. And she'd miss them dreadfully if she went away for weeks on end.

Round and round…

But something scared her even more than relocating to a country crammed with cuckoo clocks. Was she actually good enough? What if Madame von Berne had made a terrible error? What if she'd forgotten her contact lenses that morning at the rink and had failed to spot that Frankie had two left skates? What if Frankie arrived in Switzerland to find that the other skaters could do triple toe-loops in their sleep? What if she sprawled on the ice in front of them? What if they *laughed* at her?

What then?

Round and round…

She could refuse the offer. She could say, "*Sorry, Madame von Berne, I'm not ready for world-class tuition and international fame. I'd rather muddle about on the ice at Lee Valley. Thanks all the same.*"

Round and round and round…

It was a no-brainer, really.

The relief of making a decision was unbelievable.

Frankie slowed and stopped spinning, gliding effortlessly towards the barrier. At the last moment, she swooped away from the edge and concentrated on making long, even strokes as she did circuits of the rink. She was grinning so widely that the freezing air chilled her teeth as she zoomed alongside the barrier, her right foot instinctively crossing over the left as she skated in swift, anticlockwise circles.

"*Wheeeeeeee!*" she cried.

Breathlessly, Frankie came to a neat stop and made her way to the spectator seats. Here, she could still see the ice, its surface decorated with the passionate patterns she'd just made. By now, more skaters had arrived – young, not-so-young, some quite accomplished, others in constant danger of careering out of control. She remembered just what it was like to be a beginner.

Frankie thought back to her first time on the ice. It was during a school trip to the Lee Valley Ice Rink, seven years ago. She and her class had adored every minute – giggling and shrieking as they skidded about the ice like ungainly ducks in winter. By the end, Frankie was the only girl not holding on to the sides. (None of the boys were holding on either, but as they were piled in a rugby-style scrum, that didn't count.) But not only had she waved goodbye to the sides, she was upright too and skating fast, oblivious to everyone around her.

When others called her a show-off, she was totally astonished. She didn't *do* showing-off. Wouldn't *dream* of it! If anything, Frankie would go out of her way to escape the limelight. She was just enjoying herself, that was all – enjoying herself more than she ever had before.

Frankie had fallen in love with the ice.

The next time she skated, Frankie made sure that none of her classmates were about. It took a colossal amount of grovelling and faithful promises to wash up until she was about 103, but Mum relented at last. One Saturday – early enough to qualify for the cheap entrance fee – Mum took her back to the Lee Valley Ice Rink.

Skating was just as brilliant as Frankie remembered. In fact, without the catcalling of her envious classmates, it was way better. She hadn't a clue what she was doing and just made it up as she went along, knowing instinctively that a little pressure here and a push there would turn her the way she wanted to go.

Even Mum was impressed. "Where did you learn to do that?" she asked.

"I didn't," said Frankie honestly. "My feet just seem to know what to do."

"Right," Mum replied, nodding uncertainly as if she didn't really have a clue what her daughter meant.

Frankie had known without asking that lessons were out of the question – everything about ice skating seemed to be ludicrously expensive – but she wasn't upset; far from it. She borrowed books on technique from the library and glued herself to the television whenever figure skating was shown, replaying the routines over and over again to watch how the stars actually did the moves. She listened to the commentators, soon figuring out the difference between a pull-up spin and an inside spread eagle. It was like learning a whole new language, but *so* much better than French.

Then, whenever she got the chance, she tried out

all she'd learned at the ice rink. Sometimes it worked like a dream and she'd fly across the ice. Usually, she came to earth with a bump. Dad joked that her behind must look like a Rembrandt painting, she fell on it so often. She wasn't put off though. It would take more than bruises to stop her skating.

"Why do you like it so much?" Mum asked one Saturday, astonished by the sheer number of times she'd tried – and failed – the fiendishly difficult one-footed spin.

Frankie had shrugged. "Dunno." It was something she found impossible to explain. She wasn't sure she even understood it herself. Maybe it was because when she was off the ice, she was just plain average – average height and build, average hair (brown), average eyes (green) and skin that warranted a sun protection factor of at least thirty. On the ice, it was a different story. She didn't feel average. She felt a million dollars. *She loved it!*

If she had been in charge, Frankie would have skated all day, every day, but real life got in the way and she was lucky if she made it to the rink once a month. Then, on her twelfth birthday, Dad blew her out of the water with his incredible plan. His route took him very close to the Lee Valley Ice Rink, right? So, IF she could get up in time and IF she went straight to school afterwards (and did not pass GO, did not collect £200, etc., etc.) and IF she didn't talk to strangers while she was there and IF her schoolwork didn't suffer…IF and ONLY IF she satisfied all these criteria and any more that occurred to him, he would drop her at the ice rink. But she'd have to pay for it out of her own pocket money and birthday money.

Frankie was speechless with delight.

To her parents' complete astonishment, she took Dad at his word and went to the ice rink every single day, apart from Sundays, when they both had a well-deserved day off. She could put in all the practice she wanted, revelling in the early-morning emptiness of the rink. But even though she now spent more time at Lee Valley than ever before, nothing had really changed. It wasn't enough. The ice kept calling her back for more.

"Oi!"

With a jolt, Frankie landed back in the present,

back to the hard, plastic chair that was making her bottom go numb. The rink was empty now. All the skaters had vanished, to be replaced by the Zamboni.

"If you sit there much longer, I'll start charging you rent!" Harry, the friendly old man who smoothed the rink with the ice-resurfacing machine, slid past in a flurry of noise. He gave her a cheery wave. "That posh lass – the one with the tartan suit and the helmet hair," he shouted. "Did she find you? She was watching you like a hawk yesterday morning. Scribbling stuff in a little notebook and taking photos on her mobile... She was here for hours. I think I overheard her asking for you at reception."

Frankie nodded. "She found me."

"What did she want?"

"She offered to take me to Switzerland so I could train as part of the junior Olympic team," Frankie called back.

Harry guffawed. "Nice one!" he shouted. "You're funny, you know that? What did she *really* want?"

With a grin, Frankie slung her ice skates over her

shoulder and padded in stockinged feet back to the changing room, waving to Harry as she went. He didn't believe it, but neither did she. Not really.

She was going to have to get her head round it soon, though.

Out there on the ice, the place she felt most at home in the entire world, she'd made up her mind. She was going to accept Madame Kristiana von Berne's amazing offer. She was going to Switzerland. She was going to train with Team GB. And if she was good enough, Frankie was going to the next Winter Olympics. She would be one of the youngest competitors *ever*.

CHAPTER *Three*

"Is it true?" Lauren demanded, tapping Frankie on the shoulder.

It was Monday again and they were in an English lesson, trying to work out whether the answer to the question scribbled on the board was "if I was" or "if I were", while the teacher hunted for more dictionaries in the storeroom. Today was the day that Frankie had decided to tell everyone, but it sounded as if someone had already blabbed the good news.

"They're all talking about it, you know, about you moving to Switzerland to join a yodelling choir. I told them not to be stupid. You wouldn't do anything weird like that."

Frankie blushed and exchanged glances with Rosie, her best friend since for ever, who of course knew everything. "It *is* true," she mumbled to Lauren. "Well, not the bit about yodelling, but I am going to Switzerland – to train as a figure skater."

Lauren's eyebrows shot up. "No!" she said.

"Er…yes."

"Cool."

Frankie attempted a smile, like the ones she'd been practising in the bathroom mirror for when she was famous. It was meant to be a happy, confident and gracious smile, but really it just looked as if she had a stomach ache from eating too many sweets.

"Are you all right?" asked Rosie.

"Just nervous," admitted Frankie, hoping that no one was listening in. She was usually so quiet that, with the exception of Rosie and a couple of other girls, most of her classmates just left her alone. Frankie wasn't one of the popular ones that chattered incessantly about clothes and iPods and where they would be pierced if they were allowed. To everyone else, she was just "the quiet one". Only last week, during break time, the meaner girls had voted her "person least likely to become famous".

So it was hardly surprising that Lauren was gobsmacked now. "Psssst!" she hissed to the girl in front. "Did you hear about Frankie? She's going to be an ice skater!"

"A nice skater?" said Alfie, looking up from his book in confusion.

"No...*ice* skater," Rosie said proudly – and very loudly. "Frankie's going to Switzerland to train with Team GB. She's going to be a figure skater!"

Two things happened at the same time. Mrs. Skinner returned to the classroom with a teetering pile of books and the chattering students fell silent – apart from Rosie, whose comments had been broadcast loud and clear.

Frankie's cheeks burning at the unwanted publicity, she sank down in her seat, as low as she could go.

"Frankie Wills," said the English teacher.

Apparently, she hadn't gone low enough.

"Mmm?" Frankie raised her head and gave a tentative smile. To her utter astonishment, the English teacher beamed back.

"I've just heard the wonderful news," Mrs. Skinner said. "I had no idea we had such a star in our midst. And you're off to Switzerland? What a fantastic opportunity!"

Luckily, the teacher didn't seem to require any response from Frankie, who just nodded back. Encouraged by Mrs. Skinner's jovial mood, the rest of the class began to join in, firing question after question at the new star.

"Can you skate on one foot?"

"Do you have a Lycra sequinned dress with a see-through back?"

"What about those long ribbons? Do you trail those after you?"

Lauren, suddenly Frankie's self-styled expert, tutted. "That's gymnastics, stupid."

"Can you spin on your head?"

Everyone turned to look at Ben, who shrugged.

"I just wondered…" he said, his voice trailing away.

Her teeth bared in a ferocious smile, Mrs. Skinner marched to the back of the class, where Frankie cowered, hoping upon hope that a meteorite would land on the desk or someone would discover a cure for the common cold or anything at all would happen that would divert attention away from her. The last thing she wanted was to be dragged to the front of the classroom and suffer some tortuous show-and-tell session about her new life.

It wasn't her lucky day.

"Why don't you come to the front?" said Mrs. Skinner, so close that Frankie could count the hairs poking out of her teacher's cavernous nostrils. "It's almost home time. You can tell us *all* about it before we go."

"It could have been worse, I suppose," said Frankie, her face frozen into the expression of pure terror that she'd worn ever since her unwanted promotion from Class Nobody to Class Somebody Special.

"They could have put me in stocks and thrown rotten tomatoes at me. Or dangled me by my feet over a pool of hungry sharks." She took a calming slurp of tea. "Actually…I think I would have preferred that. We've all got to write an essay entitled *If I were an Olympic champion*, you know? Because of me!"

Mum patted her shoulder. "You'll have to get used to audiences, dear," she said. "What about when you compete on the ice? I don't think they'll let you perform in an empty stadium."

"But that's *different*," said Frankie. She tried to explain. "When I'm skating, it's like I'm alone. It's just me. I forget that anything else exists."

Her mum nodded understandingly, giving Frankie her umpteenth hug of the day. Since she'd told them that she really would be going, Mum and Dad couldn't even pass her on the stairs without hugging her. Whenever she left the house, it was like she was emigrating.

"It won't be the same when you're gone," said Mum, sniffing. "The house will be so *quiet* without you."

THUD! Thud-thud-thud. Thud-*thud*.

Either Joshua was hurling his bedroom furniture around the room or he was coming down the stairs.

Mum wrenched open the living-room door. "What have I told you about wearing those boots in the house?" she shouted. "Look at the mud!"

Woken from her afternoon nap, Jess began to wail.

Meg joined in.

"What's with the dreadful *racket*?" yelled Dad, home from work. He slammed the front door behind him. "Can't I get a moment's peace around here?"

Frankie smiled to herself. Whatever else Mum might miss when she'd gone to Switzerland, it wouldn't be the lack of noise.

"Hi there, love. Good day at school?" Dad didn't wait for a response. He was far too interested in the contents of the biscuit tin. "I spoke to that woman this morning," he said, looking up suddenly. His eyebrows bunched together, a sure sign that he was gearing up for a Dad Joke. "Madame Bernie

Ecclestone, or whatever she's called." He smiled at the riotous applause from his imaginary audience.

Frankie groaned. "Hilarious, Dad. What did she want?"

"She wants you to call her," he replied. "Something to do with ice…ah, yes, ice skating. That was it. And flights. She managed to fast-track your visa application and book you on the Saturday flight."

"*What?*" Frankie's screeched reply mingled with her mother's to create a sound that would have perforated eardrums, if anyone in the Wills household had had any still intact. "*This* Saturday?" She counted quickly on her fingers. "The Saturday that's only *five days away*?"

Dad nodded. "That's what she said."

"We have so much to do!" cried Mum, thrusting a twin at her husband and hustling Frankie out of the room and up the stairs, all while babbling incoherently about toothpaste, woolly hats and fleeces.

As for Frankie, she felt a mixture of fear and excitement. She was leaving her home, family and friends – for what? A dream that had only the tiniest chance of coming true. But while there was a chance – however small – of being an Olympic champion, she had to go for it.

Because, one day, it just might come true.

CHAPTER *Four*

To: RosieP
From: Frankieonthemove
Subject: Burble alert!!!

Hi Rosie!

Help! Everything's gone weird! And everyone's gone weird, too.

Like Mum, for instance. Usually, she'd go ballistic if she found my uniform in a heap. Today, she hugged my school jumper and buried her face in it as if it'd been drenched in her favourite perfume.

Dad's being super-soppy. He made this long-winded speech last night about how he might not be my real dad, but he was as proud as a real dad could be and, well, he went to "sort out his socket set" at that point, so I never found out what else he wanted to say. Josh offered to download some new tracks onto my iPod, which has got to be the most useful thing he's ever done in the history of brotherly annoyance. He even said he'd avoid any of his weirdo bands that no one's ever heard of, though I'll believe that when I don't hear it.

I feel really odd now I've said goodbye to you and everyone else at school. Did you see how all the popular girls were flocking round me, asking if I could get them tickets for the Winter Olympics? That was mega-weird… I told them that I'd reserve the Royal Box, just to shut them up. I doubt they'll remember me next week. Mind you, I doubt there is a Royal

Box. If there is, though, there'll be space in it for you!

So, I'm packed and I'm about to set off on the most incredible adventure of my entire life. And I'm bricking it. What if Madame von Wotsit realizes that she's made a huge mistake?

What if I'm RUBBISH?

Love,

Frankie X

PS I'll miss you!

Frankie hit *Send*. Then she grabbed a pen to start writing luggage labels, but began sucking it furiously instead. She simply couldn't believe that Madame Kristiana von Berne had really picked her. Perhaps there had been the most terrible mix-up and when she arrived at the Ice Palace – as she'd secretly nicknamed the training school – she would be exposed as being no better than a Z-list celebrity skater from the telly!

"Ewww!"

A curious metallic wetness flooded her mouth

and Frankie realized that, in her anxiety, she'd crunched clean through the plastic pen.

"Ack!"

She rushed to the bathroom and stuck out her very, very blue tongue.

"You look like an alien," observed Josh, "or a cow with that disease." He pushed past her to grab a bottle from the cabinet. "Ready for the last supper?" He sprayed himself liberally until the air was pungent with Dad's best aftershave.

"Urgh!"

"You really ought to broaden your vocabulary," said Josh primly. "Use proper words sometimes." He skipped to one side, cleverly anticipating Frankie's right hook, and stuck out his beautifully pink tongue, before slamming the door behind him.

She heard him clattering down the stairs, claiming loudly that Frankie thought Dad's taste in aftershave was rubbish. But for once, she wasn't cross with her brother. Not even slightly. Instead, she grabbed a toothbrush and loaded it with toothpaste, before scrubbing at her poor, stained tongue. By the time she arrived downstairs, now wearing her newest jeans and sparkly top, the indigo had been softened to a more pleasing lilac. The entire family was waiting by the front door, complaining loudly that they were starving and couldn't wait to get to the restaurant.

Frankie saw with surprise that Dad had abandoned his cords and cardigan for a suit – a suit! – and Mum was wearing her favourite floaty frock that she reserved for weddings. The twins were clad in red, to make any tomato-sauce accidents less noticeable. And Josh was wearing black, not because he was mourning her departure, but because that was what he always wore.

Their destination was Roderigo's, the local trattoria. That was where they always went on special occasions. Even though everyone knew that Roderigo was really called Roger, and that he came from Walthamstow, not Naples, it didn't make the food any less delicious. And if Frankie squinted a bit, it was just like being in Italy. Probably.

"Ready, m'lady?" asked Dad, offering his arm.

Frankie nodded, suddenly realizing that she *was*

ready. She was ready for a riotous last evening with her family. She was ready for her life in the Swiss Alps.

She was ready for anything.

Before she knew it, Frankie's alarm was beeping her into wakefulness and telling her it was Saturday. Blearily, she peered at the bright green numbers.

5.00 a.m.

Ouch! It was even earlier than usual.

Strangely, the alarm clock seemed to have banished the dreamlike quality of the past few days, and the feeling of dread that had lodged itself in the pit of her stomach had been replaced by a sense of bubbling anticipation. With surprise, Frankie realized that she was… She paused to check. No, really? Could she be? Yes! She was actually *excited*.

She tumbled out of bed, flicked on the light and peeked at herself in the heart-shaped mirror she'd had since she was seven. Was it her imagination, or did she look a little more like an Olympic medallist today? Frankie grinned at her reflection, which immediately returned the favour, the smile oozing encouragement.

"Breakfast!" Mum croaked sleepily, interrupting the grin fest. "You'd better get a wriggle on – the flight leaves in five hours!"

It sounded like a long time, but Frankie knew that once the extreme faffing for which her family was renowned was under way, the time would disappear quicker than chocolate from Mum's not-so-secret stash.

It went even faster.

Before Frankie knew it, they were at Heathrow, balancing her bulging suitcase on a trolley. It looked very lonely there, as if it were missing the pyramid of luggage belonging to the rest of the family. Frankie, who'd managed to remain calm until now, choked back a sob.

"You all right?" asked her brother. He patted her shoulder awkwardly.

Frankie nodded, not trusting herself to speak. She'd never flown solo before and she suddenly felt daunted and horribly nervous. She might have a chaperone to accompany her, but the chaperone was a stranger too.

"Hey, there's your flight!" said Dad, jabbing a finger towards the overhead display. Airports were second only to the London Transport Network in terms of pure excitement, as far as he was concerned. He loved everything about them, from the constant bing-bonging of announcements to the overpriced coffee. Queues were just a chance to get to know his fellow passengers better. He nearly foamed at the mouth if he were ever asked to empty his hand luggage. Today was no exception, as he eagerly pointed out the drop-off point for oversized bags and told Frankie how many centimetres of leg room she'd have. It was only after they'd watched her bag sail away on the conveyor belt at check-in that what was happening really sank in.

"So, you're really going, then," said Dad in a small voice.

"Yep." Frankie nodded, hoping that she wasn't going to embarrass everyone with tears. She needn't have worried – Mum beat her to it, wailing loudly into a too-small paper hankie. And really, it was only polite for Frankie to join in.

Soon, they were all snivelling, with the exception of Josh, who remained calm in the face of his family's hysteria. "She's just going to Switzerland," he whispered to Mum. "Not outer space."

"I know," sobbed Mum. "But it's for so lo-o-o-ong."

"Only eight weeks," said Josh reasonably. "And just think how much showing off you can do when she's an Olympic champion." He gave his mum a quick hug.

"Josh is right," said Frankie, sniffing hard. "Eight weeks and I'll be back for the British Junior Championships in London, remember? If I'm good enough, that is."

Mum brightened immediately.

The British Junior Championships might not be as glitzy or as high profile as other prestigious events like the World Figure Skating Championships or the Winter Olympics, but they were very important in the world of figure skating. Madame had said that they gave younger skaters the chance to take part in a real competition, but without the huge pressures associated with larger, scarier events. And it gave all the experts a chance to check out the up-and-coming talent.

"And we can come along and watch, can't we?" said Dad.

"Of course," said Frankie, at once feeling shy. She thought back to her brief, businesslike, but oh-so-exciting telephone conversation with Madame at the beginning of the week. She still couldn't quite believe that the coaching director wanted her to take part. "It's just a national event," Frankie explained. "But there are all the usual disciplines – singles, pairs and ice dance – and Madame says that it'll be excellent practice. I just hope she thinks I'm good enough by then." She was doing her best to forget about that last bit. She had to be good enough. Otherwise, she could wave goodbye to any chance at the Olympics. And she'd be back home before Christmas, for good.

"Oooooh!" said Jess, with excellent timing.

"Couldn't have said it better myself," said Dad. "That gold medal's got your name on it—" A well-timed *bing-bong* interrupted him mid-flow, calling

Frankie's flight. "That's you!" he said cheerily.

"I have to go," she said, quickly grabbing her rucksack before things could get emotional again. For once, there was no queue at the security barrier and, after hugs all round, she shimmied back and forth between the rope barriers, at last reaching the desk. The chaperone was waiting for her, holding a card with her name on it.

"Frankie?" called Mum.

She looked back at her family, gathered beyond the waves of ropes. She'd never been away from them for longer than a week before (a particularly wet and dismal week in Bognor with the Guides). She was going to miss them *so* much.

"Let us know as soon as you get there!" shouted Mum. "And stick to the chaperone like glue."

"Yes, Mum!"

"And don't forget to look out for a cuckoo clock!"

Frankie grinned. With a final wave, she shouldered her rucksack and followed the chaperone, who introduced herself as Serena, around the corner. Her family disappeared from sight.

"We'd better hurry," said Serena briskly.

Frankie looked at her watch. Crumbs! The farewells had taken longer than she'd realized. There were now only twenty minutes to go before her flight closed. Serena whisked them both through security and through the busy airport terminal, hopping on and off moving walkways and dodging other passengers as they went. In no time at all, they reached the gate and scurried onto the plane.

Although Serena never left her side for a moment, Frankie was now in unfamiliar territory. She was on her own. And as the plane powered upwards, slicing through wispy clouds, she had the strangest feeling… With every second, her old life was getting smaller and further away, like the runway. Her family was becoming less real, as if they were turning into the illustrations in a picture book. And at the same time, her new life was drawing closer. Her long-cherished dream of being a real figure skater was losing its haziness, edges were sharpening, becoming more and more substantial.

Very soon, it would be real.

But even as she made her way through Zurich airport, feeling very cosmopolitan indeed despite having a chaperone, she still couldn't quite register what was happening. Not even when she spotted the taxi driver holding a white board with her name printed neatly upon it did the truth sink in. It was only when the cab left the wide motorway and began its ascent up narrow zigzagging roads that she really began to believe it.

She, Frankie Wills, was going to train to be a real figure skater.

With growing excitement, she gazed at the craggy mountains on either side of the car. Then, each time they swung hard left around the next tight bend, she found herself peering down into the valley far below. It was a good job she didn't suffer from vertigo, because it was a long way down.

They passed quaint villages, with chalet-style homes hugging the side of the road. Patches of snow appeared here and there – hardly surprising, really. This wasn't a country that took bets on whether there would be a white Christmas or not.

The taxi lurched left, along an even narrower road that continued to climb, before levelling out into a valley nestled among the slopes. As the car rounded yet another bend, Frankie saw a cluster of low, white buildings at the head of the valley. The taxi slowed and stopped in front of them.

Biting her lip nervously, Frankie got out of the car. She had arrived at the Ice Palace.

CHAPTER *Five*

To: mumndadnjoshnjessnmeg
From: Frankieonthemove
Subject: I'm here!

Hello from Switzerland!

Switzerland is beautiful, like something out of a car advert – all zigzag roads and amazing scenery. But it's SO cold! The weather is below freezing already and it's only September. As for the Ice Palace, it's stunning.

I'm totally loving it already!

Big sloppy hugs,

Frankie

PS The flight was cool. Not a bit of turbulence and a great landing, despite the crosswind.

Frankie wished she felt as confident as her e-mail sounded. She knew that her parents would worry if she gave away even the slightest hint of nerves, so she was resorting to the age-old tactic of Lying Through Her Teeth, apart from the bit about the flight (which she knew Dad would love) and the amazing scenery (which would thrill her mum).

"Thank you," she said to the school secretary, who'd introduced herself as Rosalie and kindly let her e-mail home as soon as she arrived.

Rosalie smiled at her. "How about I direct you to the common room?" she said helpfully. "Leave your luggage here for now. The others will be dying to meet you, I'm sure."

"Great," said Frankie, hoping that if she showed enough teeth when she smiled, the woman might really believe that she was actually looking forward to it.

It was like being the last person to arrive at a party. Frankie wasn't even sure if anyone had noticed her, let alone if they liked her or not. When she crept into the common room, there was barely a raised eyebrow to acknowledge her arrival. It was like she was invisible. She seriously began to wonder if she *was*.

Beneath lowered lashes, Frankie's eyes flicked left and right to take it all in. The room was dotted with squashy sofas and beanbags and tastefully decorated in muted shades of stone and ice-blue. Luckily, the walls were smothered with tatty posters of figure skaters past and present, to reassure her that this wasn't a furniture shop. Frankie felt a wave of homesickness. This was light years from her own cosy home. (Technically, 780 kilometres as the crow flies – but it might as well have been a million.)

There were perhaps thirty young people here. One or two looked the same age as her, but others were way older. Most were clustered in small groups, engrossed in earnest discussions.

A girl wearing a bright pink velour tracksuit came over first.

"Hello!" said the girl cheerily. The initials FB were monogrammed on her lapel. And she oozed money.

Frankie's spirits rose. "Hello," she said bravely. "I'm new."

"I know that, stupid," replied the girl, rolling her eyes. "I'm Felicity Brightman. My friends call me Flic."

Frankie was too mesmerized by the girl's beautifully curled and mascaraed eyelashes – *were they false?* – to realize immediately that Flic had paused for a reason.

"And you are?" she prompted.

"Oh, I'm Frankie," she gabbled, reddening. "My friends call me, er…Frankie. I'm new."

"You said," replied Flic. She inspected her with narrowed eyes.

Frankie could imagine what Flic saw – a fourteen-year-old girl whose parents were not wealthy enough to afford the latest gear. A girl whose hair wasn't highlighted, wasn't straightened, wasn't even painstakingly coiffed into a just-got-out-of-bed look. It was just brown and a bit messy. What Frankie didn't know was why the girl was looking at her so strangely. But it soon became clear.

"Hey, Scarlett!" Flic said loudly. "She's here. It's Madame's little skating star – the one we've heard so much about. You know, the natural? The one who's never had a proper lesson?"

A doll-like girl with long blonde hair and cherry-pink cheeks looked over from the other side of the common room. She wore a powder-blue velour tracksuit very like Flic's. "*Her?*" she said incredulously. She glared at Frankie, not even trying to hide her dislike. "This is the new Olympic champion? I thought she'd at least *look* like a figure skater. She's no Katarina Witt, is she?"

"Scarlett Jones!" snapped a tall girl with a mane of beautiful black hair and ebony skin. Frankie was incredibly relieved to see that she wasn't wearing a velour tracksuit. "I've never heard anything so mean!" She turned to Frankie and smiled warmly.

Scarlett tutted. "So-rry," she drawled, not looking apologetic in the slightest.

"Shhhhh!" hissed a dark-haired boy. "Madame's coming!"

The crowd that had gathered round the newcomer quickly returned to their original huddles, where they began to discuss jumps and tucks in loud, false voices.

Madame von Berne didn't seem to register the strained atmosphere. Her heels tapping like an overworked metronome, she strode briskly to the centre of the common room and clapped her hands together. "May I have your attention, please!" she said.

Frankie, still reeling from Scarlett's snide comment, observed that there was an immediate hush. It didn't take a rocket scientist to work out that Madame von Berne was feared *and* revered around here. Every single pair of eyes was fixed upon the woman, as they waited for her next words.

"I would like to introduce a new team member to you all," said the diminutive teacher. She waved in Frankie's direction and gestured that she should stand up. Inwardly quaking, Frankie obeyed, her eyes focused firmly on the floor. She'd seen their accusing stares once. She didn't need reminding. "This is Frankie Wills," said Madame von Berne.

"We're so pleased to meet you," said a friendly voice. Nervously, Frankie raised her eyes to see that the girl who'd scolded Scarlett had spoken. What's more, she sounded as if she meant it. "I'm Marianne," she said, smiling.

Frankie couldn't help returning the smile. "Hi," she said quietly. Then she flinched as a deafening chorus of "Hello"s and "Hi"s and "How-are-you?"s came right back at her. A boy with dark-red floppy hair gave her a huge wink that made her blush.

"That's more like it," Marianne murmured, too low for the coach to hear. Frankie felt a huge rush of gratitude.

"Frankie will be receiving one-to-one tuition from me, to begin with," Madame von Berne went on. "Until she's up to speed, that is. Her ice-skating career so far has been rather…unstructured. But she will also take part in group sessions and will join you for lessons too. Do your best to make her feel at home." The coach pulled out a small notebook and flipped it open. "Ah, yes. There's a spare bed for you in one of the smaller dormitories, Frankie. You will be sharing with…"

Frankie held her breath and wished as hard as she could. Please, please, please let it *not* be Scarlett Jones.

"…Scarlett Jones," said Madame von Berne. "And…"

Great. She was sharing with the girl who obviously thought she was a nobody. But at least she wasn't in the same room as Felicity Brightman.

"…Felicity Brightman," said the coach. "And…" She paused, looking closely at the notebook.

Frankie reasoned that it couldn't really get any worse. Not unless they'd shipped in Dracula from Transylvania to be her room-mate. Or the Wicked Witch of the West.

"…Alesha Pattinson," Madame finished. She scanned the common room, her icy-blue eyes coming to rest on a girl with dark eyes outlined in kohl and fashionably ruffled dark hair. She too had spurned the velour tracksuit in favour of jeans and a hoodie. "Ah, there you are. Alesha, can you give Frankie the guided tour?"

"Sure," said the girl, barely looking up from her magazine. "Right away." She flicked over the page and carried on reading.

"Splendid," said the coach. "Then I'll see you all at dinner. Frankie, you'll meet the rest of the teaching staff then." She spun round and tip-tapped away.

The room began to buzz with noise once more, but as soon as the coach had gone, Frankie pretended to be engrossed in her book again. She could guess that Scarlett and Felicity would be as overjoyed as she was about the room-mate situation and she couldn't bear to witness their disgruntled reactions.

"Hey."

Frankie was surprised to see Alesha leaning nonchalantly against her armchair. "Hello," she said nervously, not really knowing what to expect from this girl who seemed so cool, she was practically sub-zero.

"Come on, then," said Alesha. "Ready for the grand tour?" Her lip curled into a lopsided smile.

And for the first time since she'd arrived, Frankie began to feel just the tiniest glimmer of hope. Perhaps it was going to be okay here after all. She leaped from the chair and followed Alesha out of the common room.

Chapter *Six*

"Don't worry about those two," drawled Alesha. The babble of voices in the common room faded to a low murmur as the door swung shut behind them. "Scarlett's a seriously good skater, but that's no excuse for being catty. She and Felicity are so full of themselves, they're bursting at the seams of their designer clothes. They'll pop with their own importance one day soon. And then won't there be a mess?"

Frankie smiled uncertainly. "You aren't best friends then?"

Alesha looked away. "It's not really the sort of place that encourages close friendships," she mumbled. "Madame sees to that." She shrugged and set off down the long corridor that led back to the entrance.

"Oh." This wasn't what Frankie needed to hear. Not right now. Not when she'd just left her family, friends, casual acquaintances, postman – *everyone she knew* – back in London. She was missing everyone already, desperately. Even the sour-faced woman who sold tickets at the ice rink.

Actually, not her. Frankie was glad to leave *her* behind.

Realizing that *she* was being left behind by her fleet-footed tour guide, Frankie raced after her. "You have *no friends*?" she gasped.

"Did I *say* that?" snapped Alesha. She glanced left and right, as if checking for eavesdroppers, then hurried through a set of double doors into a large locker room. "It's not too bad here. Forget I said anything." She gave a forced smile and pointed to a large, metal, standard-issue locker. "Here's a spare locker you can use," she said, slamming the door, plucking the key from the lock and tossing it in Frankie's direction. "Want to see the ice?"

It was clear there would be no more bean-spilling for now.

Frankie didn't care. She nodded, a nervous excitement banishing all other thoughts from her mind. The ice… The hallowed arena where dreams were made. She followed her guide through the changing room, noticing the telltale blade marks that streamed across the rubbery floor towards the exit. Alesha swung the doors open and beckoned Frankie through.

The rink was in total darkness, but a sudden chill in the air warned Frankie that she was close. There was ice nearby…

"Ready?" asked Alesha.

Was she *ready*? It was suddenly as if Frankie had waited her whole fourteen years for this moment. She croaked a "Yes", uncertain whether it was the sudden drop in temperature or the unbearable suspense that was making the hairs on the back of her neck stand up like tin soldiers.

With a magician-like sweep of her arm, Alesha

flicked a light switch. "Ta-daaaaa!"

A row of lights snapped on to illuminate a steep bank of spectator seats in the distance and Frankie gulped as she realized how far away they were. This place was *huge*. But she still couldn't quite make out the ice rink itself.

Click!

Another row of lights shone, closer now. Frankie had her first tantalizing glimpse of the ice, glowing softly in the semi-darkness. Her skin began to prickle with excitement.

With a flourish, Alesha flipped the last three switches in quick succession and a wave of brightness rushed towards them as the entire ice rink blazed with light.

"Wow," said Frankie.

Alesha grinned. Her earlier gloom seemed to have vanished now. "Is that it?" she said. "The biggest ice rink in Switzerland and all you can say is 'wow'?"

Frankie nodded. "Just…wow."

The ice stretched away from them. There was enough space here to accommodate the entire cast of *Holiday on Ice*. And all the extras. It was brilliant, literally. The high ceiling was a mass of spotlights that made the ice glow like the brightest star. A bank of blue and green seats circled the barrier, rows of them, rising up and away from the ice. There was plenty of room for a vast audience. It must be used for competitions as well as practice. For the first time ever, Frankie found herself feeling apprehensive at the thought of onlookers assessing her routine, criticizing her moves, judges awarding scores… She shuddered, concentrating instead on the ice. She could picture herself, gliding to the very centre and performing the most dazzling spin of her life. It would be a Biellmann. She would balance on one leg, extending the other behind her, up and over her head, leaning back to grasp her free skate and spinning, spinning, spinning—

"Good daydream?" asked Alesha. She was sprawling on the front row of the seats with her hood up, hugging herself for warmth. "It always has the same effect on new arrivals. Which medal did you win?"

A warm blush coloured Frankie's cheeks. "Er…
I hadn't got to the podium," she admitted. "I was
in the middle of a spin."

Alesha clambered to her feet. "Fast, was it?"

"*Supersonic*," replied Frankie.

"Cool," said Alesha, with a shiver. "Talking of
which, I'm freezing. Shall we go on?"

Frankie nodded, feeling a pang of disappointment
that they were leaving so soon. What with all the
packing, shopping and tearful goodbyes, she hadn't
skated in five days. It was pure torture to be so close
to a rink and not clock up a few basic moves. A few
crossovers was all she needed – and perhaps a
forward spiral or two. Nothing flash.

But it was not to be.

"Yoohoo!" called Alesha from the changing-
room doorway. "Earth calling Frankie! Come on.
The ice won't defrost before this evening. And
then you can show us all what you're made of."
She looked at her watch. "We'd better crack on.
Next stop, the canteen. I'm warning you, though.
It's not as awe-inspiring as this. Well, not unless
you're a celebrity chef with a mission to make sure

that future Olympic stars have their five-a-day. Then you'd just love it."

After the pure magic of the ice rink, the rest of the training school seemed strangely mundane. Canteen, classrooms, library, gym…Frankie didn't even register what they looked like and couldn't have found them again if she'd been paid. But things took a turn for the better once they got to the Ice Palace's entrance. When the taxi had deposited her there, just an hour earlier, she'd been too stunned to take it all in. Now, she stood back with jaw dropped and eyes wide. And she gawped.

It wasn't a huge entrance hall, and not especially grand either. There was no posh parquet floor, no oak panelling. Just lino and boring old cream walls. It was what was *on* the walls that made Frankie stop and stare.

"Impressive, huh?" Alesha's habitually cool expression had given way to another lopsided smile.

If she said "Wow" one more time, Frankie worried that Alesha would think she had the vocabulary of a two year old. So she settled for a half-strangled "Yes", while thinking that she must have been *really* out of it to have missed this when she arrived. Now she had her eyes truly open, Frankie realized that the entrance hall reminded her of a restaurant. One of *those* restaurants…where the walls were plastered with hundreds of photos – the owner clasping a different minor celebrity in every shot. Except, here, the photos were of ice skaters performing every imaginable jump, spin, hop and flip and many more besides.

One picture stood out from the rest. It wasn't gilt-edged or A3-sized. It wasn't even in a wooden surround, just a plain old clip-frame. But it could have been a torn scrap of newspaper and it would still have been as out-of-place as a motorbike in the Tour de France.

The skater was a woman, very petite with ebony hair. She wore a plain black dress – no frills, no sparkles, nothing. Her boots were white. She was suspended way above the ice, frozen for ever in mid-air by the camera's shutter, her arms tucked in tight, her legs crossed as she executed a perfect…

"Double toe-loop," breathed Frankie.

"Triple," corrected Alesha. "That was taken during one of her most famous routines. Copenhagen, 1982. The World Figure Skating Championships."

"Mmm." Frankie couldn't drag her eyes from the photo. This was exactly how she wanted to skate, as if she were lighter than air, performing textbook poses with the flair and finesse of an Olympic champion.

"You don't recognize her, do you?" A mischievous grin lit up Alesha's face. She looked pointedly at the photo, then back at Frankie. "Ha!"

"Course I do." There was no way Frankie was going to admit that she hadn't a clue. Not when Alesha was looking so pleased with herself. "It's Katarina Witt," she guessed.

"Yeah, right."

"Tanja Szewczenko?"

"No, and I bet you can't spell that either."

"Denise Biellmann!" announced Frankie triumphantly. Phew, she'd got it at last. The hundreds of hours of ice-skating footage that she'd absorbed had all been worth it.

"Wrong!" Alesha couldn't conceal her delight.

"*Who* then?

"Kristiana von Berne."

Frankie performed a triple-take nearly as neat as the ice skater's triple toe-loop. "You're kidding..." she said. But as she looked more closely at the grainy photo, she could see that it was true. There were the telltale arched eyebrows and the sapphire-blue eyes. "It *is* Madame!" she spluttered. And suddenly she realized why Madame Kristiana von Berne had seemed so familiar when she'd first met her. She was *that* Kristiana von Berne. One of the most promising ice skaters *ever*. How could Frankie have been so *stupid*?

"Of course it is," said Alesha. "She didn't get to be the British junior coaching director by reading library books about ice skating. Madame Kristiana von Berne was a real, true-life, no-kidding-matey, professional figure skater. And she would have been the 1982 world champion too, if she hadn't tripped before her last jump."

If she'd been about to undergo laser eye surgery, Frankie couldn't have opened her eyes any wider.

That was *dreadful*. How utterly disappointing it must have been for the coaching director to be so close to winning, only to crash out in defeat. It was every skater's worst nightmare.

"She broke her ankle so badly that she never competed again," Alesha went on, a faraway look in her eyes. "Anyway, she couldn't bear to leave the world of international figure skating and now she's the Team GB coaching director." Alesha tugged her zip right up to her chin and yanked up the hood, before leading the way out of the warm building into the chilly night air. "Let's check out the dorms," she said, loud enough for Rosalie the secretary and indeed half of Switzerland to hear. Then she lowered her voice. "I'll tell you something for nothing. She's out to win this time. And Madame Kristiana von Berne won't let her team settle for anything less than Olympic gold."

CHAPTER *Seven*

Her head was spinning with it all, which was the strangest feeling given that Frankie was nowhere near the ice.

She flopped down on her bed, relieved to be away from curious stares. Pleading jetlag – there *was* a whole sixty minutes' time difference between here and Greenwich, so Frankie figured that it was an entirely plausible excuse – she'd left the others in the common room and decided to unpack. Someone had already delivered her battered suitcase to her dorm, and now she fumbled with the ancient lock, which promptly broke in her hand. She laughed quietly and threw the lock into the bin. Apart from her scruffy old boots – and who would want *them*? – it wasn't as if she had anything worth stealing anyway.

In less time than it takes to perform a toe-loop, she'd unpacked, using the simple technique of upending the suitcase and shaking out the contents. She stuffed her clothes into the set of drawers beside her bunk bed. Naturally, it was the bottom bunk. The top bunk had already been claimed by someone who loved, and *really* loved, the colour pink. Pink duvet cover, pink bunny, pink pyjamas emblazoned with the logo *Pink to Make the Boys Wink*. It had to be Flic's bunk.

Great.

Frankie looked at her watch – 5.45 p.m. Fifteen minutes until dinner. Fifteen minutes to get her head straight. With a weary sigh, she leaned against the wall, hugged her knees and closed her eyes. Her poor, overtaxed brain instantly went beserk. She was in Switzerland…on her own… She was here to skate…to compete…and it was *such* a wonderful ice rink. She couldn't wait to get out there. But *why* were people so unfriendly? What did Alesha mean about friendships not being encouraged? *Did Frankie need to beg, borrow or steal a velour tracksuit in order to fit in?*

Deep breaths… In through the nose and out through the mouth. In…out…in…out. Caaaaalm.

That was better.

What did Frankie's old English teacher tell her to do before writing an essay? Make a list of salient points. Right. She'd do that to get her head straightened out.

1. She was on the brink of a glittering skating career!
2. She was in Switzerland.
3. Her fellow skaters hadn't been over-friendly…
4. …But with the exception of Scarlett and Flic, they hadn't really been openly hostile either. So that was good, she supposed, in a negatively positive sort of way.

5. Alesha was both helpful and touchy, a curious mixture. And at least she didn't wear velour. Another plus point.
6. Point six would have to wait. It was time for tea.

Mentally filing her thoughts under *Stuff to obsess about in the small hours*, Frankie grabbed her coat and her ice skates and attempted to find her way back to the canteen. Briefly envying Hansel and Gretel their trail of bread, she eventually resorted to sniffing the air for food-based clues. Was that a whiff of Brussels sprouts, or a compost heap? She rather hoped it was the latter. It didn't matter how often Mum called them "baby cabbages" or "green jewels", she was *never* going to like them.

"Lost?"

Frankie was jolted out of her thoughts by the sight of a figure looming over her. Oooooh. The boy with the dark-red hair who had winked at her in the common room was even nicer close-up. And he wasn't too ginger, not really. More a sort of African sunset. Things were definitely looking up.

He was very tall and as willowy as, er…well, a willow tree, she supposed. Greenish eyes, longish nose, biggish mouth. Your classic hotchpotch of features that added up to a not-bad-at-all-looking lad.

Frankie realized that her mouth was hanging open. *So* not a good look. "Haven't the foggiest where I am," she said quickly. "Forgot my compass. Ha ha."

"You'll get used to it," he said, sticking out a hand and grasping hers, before pumping it up and down as if he fully expected water to shoot out of her mouth. "Dylan," he said. "But I answer to most things. Come on, I'll show you where the canteen is, before we both starve. Everyone eats there – students and trainers. Madame's doing a pep talk after dinner and then there's free skating tonight. You won't want to miss that."

Frankie could hardly eat a thing, she was so nervous. It was all she could do to choke down a couple of mouthfuls of spaghetti Bolognese, which then fermented in her stomach like warm yeast. She was staring wistfully at the treacle tart when Madame stood up and cleared her throat.

The noisy chatter ceased and Frankie marvelled anew at the respect commanded by this tiny woman. Now that she knew just how talented a skater Madame Kristiana von Berne had once been, she was beginning to understand why everyone was so awestruck.

"I'll keep it brief this evening," said Madame. "I can guess that some of you" – here, she smiled directly at the new girl – "are eager to take to the ice." There was a smattering of polite laughter and Frankie cringed, sure that everyone's attention was directed at her. She kept her eyes fixed on the melting Parmesan perched atop her spag bol until her cheeks had stopped burning.

"For the benefit of Frankie, I'd like to introduce the other Team GB coaches," continued Madame. "I'm sure Mrs. Williams and Mr. Pearson won't mind standing up for a moment?"

Obligingly, an athletic-looking woman with fiery red hair and a broad smile sprang out of her seat. "Hi there!" she shouted in Frankie's direction.

A tall man with dark skin and a shaved head rose slowly to his feet. He gave a lazy nod. "Look forward to seeing you in class, Frankie," he said in a deep, gravelly voice.

Frankie blushed, wishing that the limelight would shift to someone else in the room. By now, she was longing to fade into the shadows.

Dylan nudged her. "Don't be fooled by Rob Pearson," he said under his breath. "He's nearly as tough as Madame, despite the cool, laid-back exterior. And Ally Williams is a right laugh, until she thinks you're slacking. Then, watch out…"

Madame von Berne had starting talking again. "Can I remind you all that free skating is a time for you to relax and enjoy yourselves? That means allowing everyone to do their own thing. Okay?"

There were a few eager nods.

"Excellent," said the coaching director. "Now, I'd like you to forget about routines, forget about competitions and medals. Just don't forget to watch where you're going. And have fun!"

The scraping of chairs was deafening. No matter how apprehensive Frankie might feel, she couldn't help but be thrilled by the eagerness everyone showed to get out on the ice. It felt so good to be among people who loved to skate as much as she did. Quickly scraping her uneaten meal into the bin and adding her plate to the teetering pile, she grabbed her boot bag and tagged along with the others, keen to join in with their excitement.

"How are your layback spins coming on, Pippa?" a boy with cool, square-rimmed glasses called over his shoulder.

"Better," replied the girl behind him. She grimaced. "Madame says I just need to relax into the posture more. But how can I relax when I'm worried that I'll fall over backwards?"

"That's something I'm brilliant at," Dylan chipped in.

"Layback spins?" asked Pippa.

"No, falling over backwards!"

"Oh, ha ha," she replied, wearing a wry smile. "Very funny."

Frankie couldn't help but laugh. She followed the others into the changing room. By now, her whole body was tingling with the thrill of it all. Fumbling with her key – had her fingers suddenly turned to marshmallow? – she repeatedly jabbed it at the lock until it slid in on the fifth attempt. It was a good thing she could skate, because she'd never make it as a cat burglar.

She pulled off her trainers and tossed them into the locker, where they landed with rubbery clangs. She was close now. So close that she could feel the ice, crisp beneath her blades. She slid her feet into the old, cracked boots, lacing them as tight as her clumsy fingers could manage. Ouch. They really were starting to pinch. Putting that thought to the back of her mind, she slid off the guards. Into the locker they went.

She was ready.

Frankie had taken so long to put on her boots that the changing room was now deserted. The chattering crowd had gone. She made her way towards the swing doors, the linoleum floor cushioning her blades, muffling any noise that they might make. In the silence, Frankie felt curiously calm. As if in a dream, she pushed open the doors and made her way towards the edge of the rink.

"Whoa…" she breathed.

A beautiful scene unfolded before her eyes, skaters gliding hither and thither over the glittering ice. Frankie tracked Pippa around the ice, the petite girl weaving in and out, never breaking her stride. Her crossovers were perfect, not a blade out of place. Then – hup! – she changed direction and was travelling backwards just as smoothly.

"Yoohoo!" cried Pippa as she slid past. "Come on in. The ice is lovely!"

The spell was broken. Frankie was back at the training rink. And Pippa was right. She *so* wanted to join everyone. Her heart pounding with nerves and excitement, she moved forward, gently stepping onto the ice. She gripped the barrier, paused for a second and took a deep, steadying breath as majestic thoughts filled her mind.

She was no longer a hobby skater.

She was part of Team GB.

This was where her Olympic dream began.

Filled with a happy confidence, Frankie pushed away from the edge, stroking her blades over the ice. Left…right…left…right—

WHAM!

CHAPTER *Eight*

Frankie didn't see what hit her. All she knew was that her skates had slid from beneath her and, for a split second, she was suspended in mid-air like a cartoon character who hasn't yet realized that they've run off a cliff.

Then – *wallop!* – she fell to earth with the grace of a sack of potatoes.

"Oooh!" she whimpered quietly to herself, wriggling her limbs in turn to make sure nothing was broken. No, just a bruised bottom and a dented ego. But that was bad enough. She was confused though. All she'd been doing was skating in a straight line – nothing complicated that warranted such a tumble. Why had she fallen? Had she forgotten how to do it? Had she hit something? She didn't know *what* had happened. Frankie scrambled quickly to her feet, her eyes firmly focused on the barrier. She shuffled towards it, her blossoming confidence in tatters.

"Oi!"

Frankie stuttered to a halt. Was someone talking to her?

"Hey, new girl!"

Yes, someone *was* talking to her. Slowly, she swivelled. There, sprawled a couple of metres away – her powder-blue tracksuit matted with ice – was Scarlett Jones. Frankie cringed. Of course, it *had* to be her, didn't it? The girl who already seemed to dislike her. Brilliant. She couldn't have picked a worse target if she'd tried.

"Are you okay?" asked Frankie. She skated forward and offered a hand to the other girl. Scarlett scowled and grabbed it, yanking herself to her feet with such force that they both nearly ended up on the ice again.

"Watch it," mumbled Frankie, regaining her balance with difficulty.

Scarlett brought her face so close that Frankie could make out her tinted contact lenses. They were blue, a perfect match for the tracksuit. "No, *you* watch it!" hissed the angry girl. "How *dare* you push me over! You did it on purpose, didn't you?"

"No…" whispered Frankie. She was horrified that Scarlett could even suggest it. "I wouldn't *do* such a thing. I don't know what happened. One minute I was skating and the next—"

"You barged into me on purpose," Scarlett finished triumphantly. Her eyes narrowed. "I know your sort. Get rid of the competition and you have a better chance of winning yourself. Well, don't count on it, Frankie. I'm the star around here." She made a big show of brushing the ice from her tracksuit, before abruptly speeding away and launching straight into a butterfly jump, effortlessly propelling herself into the air, her arms extended behind her like the gossamer wings of a butterfly, before landing perfectly on the toe pick of one skate.

Frankie just stared. *That* was how she wanted to skate, like Scarlett. Because Scarlett was good. No, she was better than good. She was brilliant.

And Scarlett knew it. Seconds later, she was zooming fearlessly around the rink, her movements as fluid as silk. She didn't appear to be at all shaken by the fall. If anything, she looked pleased.

Frankie drew a shaky breath. Suddenly, her eyes swam with so many tears that she couldn't see straight. Was anyone watching? Were they sniggering about the accident and muttering about Madame's huge mistake in bringing Frankie here? Quickly, she turned her back on the ice and hugged the barrier. She was embarrassed enough without anyone seeing her crying too.

"Hey!"

She hastily dragged her sleeve across her face and gave a mighty sniff before swivelling round.

It was Alesha, wearing a look of real concern. "Are you okay?" she asked anxiously. "Only, I saw you fall. You went down with quite a clatter."

"Uh-huh." It was all Frankie could say without bawling like a toddler. She bared her teeth in rough approximation of a smile and hoped Alesha wouldn't notice her blotchy face.

"Don't cry," said Alesha softly. "I've been here a year, the same as Scarlett. And I've seen her do that to everyone just as soon as they arrive. She even tried it on with me. Charges her victim like a battering ram and then – let me guess… Did she blame you for pushing her over?"

"Uh-huh," repeated Frankie, too astonished to be angry. So she hadn't fallen. She'd been *pushed*!

"Classic Scarlett," said Alesha, with a slow nod. "She might be a world-class skater, but she can't stand anyone else being good too." Alesha's disgruntled look returned with a vengeance and Frankie began to suspect that something rather major had happened between this pair. "Don't let her upset you," she went on, attempting a smile. "That's what she wants. And if you let it throw you off balance, that means she's won. Do you see?"

Frankie gulped loudly. Did she see *what* exactly?

All she saw was that everyone she'd met seemed to be stuck-up or paranoid or just plain weird – with the exception of her new friend Alesha, of course. And the lovely Dylan. Her eyes scanned the rink until she spotted him performing a rather neat Choctaw, changing direction and edges with a relaxed ease. He really did move beautifully on the ice. And he wasn't too bad off it either. Vaguely, she became aware of Alesha speaking, and she reluctantly tugged her attention away from Dylan.

By now, Alesha was looking rather anxious. She held up a finger and moved it left and right in front of Frankie's eyes. "Did you bonk your head when you fell? Any blurred vision?"

Frankie was suddenly struck by the sheer ridiculousness of the situation. Here she was, surrounded by skaters so determined to win that one of them was prepared to resort to bully-girl tactics. And if she allowed herself to be manipulated by her, then Frankie was a bigger fool than all of them. The urge to giggle welled up inside her and she began to shake with mirth. "I'm fine," she reassured a worried-looking Alesha. "Just got a bit of a shock, that's all. I thought I'd left playground tactics behind at school."

Alesha gave a wry smile. "Everyone's desperate to succeed here," she said. "But some are more desperate than others. Remember that."

Frankie rubbed her behind and winced. "I will," she said. "Every time I sit down."

"Come on, then." The dark-eyed girl held out her hand and Frankie grasped it thankfully. "Fancy a spin around the ice?"

"Ha! You pair have something in common," sneered Scarlett as she curved around them in a perfect pull-up spiral. "Neither of you can skate."

Vaguely wondering why Scarlett was having a dig at Alesha too, Frankie blocked out the taunting and grabbed hold of her new friend's hand. They skated away from the barrier, increasing power with every stroke. This time, it was different. Frankie felt as if she were floating on air. She barely registered when Alesha released her hand and vanished towards the outer reaches of the rink.

Frankie was on her own.

Whoosh! She launched forward on her left foot,

lifting her right foot behind her and taking care not to bend her knee as she lowered her upper body towards the ice. From her head to her toe, she formed a perfectly straight line. The forward spiral felt unbelievably good. Now she remembered why she'd come to Switzerland. Because of the skating.

Building up speed once more, she attempted another forward spiral, on her right foot this time. Feeling much more confident now, she continued to lift her left leg behind her until it was parallel with the ice – and then she went for it. Up, up, up it went. When she could push it no further, Frankie made sure that her back was arched and her arms outstretched. She held the pose for as long as she could, curving gently to the right before lowering her leg and performing a neat hockey stop beside the barrier.

"I see."

The words were spoken so softly, Frankie wasn't quite sure if she'd heard them at all. She looked over the barrier and saw Madame von Berne sitting in the front row of seats. The coach wore a vibrant scarlet pashmina, skinny jeans, riding boots made of expensive-looking caramel leather and an impenetrable expression.

Frankie's mouth was dry. What did "I see" mean exactly? *What* had Madame seen? Had she seen the potential that Frankie had displayed at Lee Valley Ice Rink? Or had she seen Frankie wipe out?

"I see…" repeated Madame in the same low, confidential tone.

Frankie relaxed. At least if she was going to be thrown out, Madame was going to do it quietly. Excellent. She didn't like a lot of fuss.

"A long way from perfect," said the coach, flipping open her trusty notebook.

Oh dear. This wasn't encouraging. Mentally, Frankie started to pack her suitcase. She could be done in under two minutes if she put her mind to it.

"Rather a shaky start, in fact."

Okay, she was getting the message.

"Your back leg wasn't anywhere near high enough and your arms were as floppy as overcooked spaghetti."

Was there any need to rub it in?

"But…" Madame von Berne paused just long enough for Frankie's heart to lift fractionally. "Not bad." And then she allowed herself a smile. Nothing flash. But it was a smile nonetheless.

"I'll see you on the ice at eight o'clock sharp tomorrow morning," the coaching director said, artfully tossing her bright pashmina over her shoulder. She got to her feet and prepared to leave.

"Wait," whispered Frankie. She'd travelled nearly a thousand kilometres. She'd made friends *and* enemies. She'd slammed into the ice with the grace of a rhinoceros. And she'd undergone a nail-biting assessment from Madame herself. All since breakfast. She was utterly, totally and completely exhausted.

"Yes?" asked Madame. She snapped shut her notebook.

"Thank you."

Madame nodded. "Here. Eight o'clock," she repeated. "Sharp."

As she watched the woman leave, Frankie's weary gaze snagged on Scarlett, who was glaring her way. Anger would have been understating things.

The girl looked truly thunderous, her expression dark and filled with foreboding. She was flanked by Flic and a dark-haired girl wearing the trademark velour zip-up top (a sickly shade of violet, this time). Another member of the stuck-up gang.

Just great.

Sudden waves of tiredness and homesickness threatened to engulf Frankie completely. She looked at her watch, astonished to see that the hour's free skate was almost up. With no desire for a cosy changing-room chat with Scarlett and her cohorts, she decided to make a quick exit.

By the time everyone else came to bed, Frankie was sound asleep.

CHAPTER *Nine*

To: mumndadnjoshnjessnmeg
From: Frankieonthemove
Subject: The hills are alive with the sound of skating!

Guten Tag!

It's my first full day and I've already officially decided that life at Skate School is bizarre. Here we are, holed up in one of the most gorgeous places on earth, and no one seems to take the slightest bit of notice of anything outside the Ice Palace. We could be in Slough for all they care. But I'm beginning to see why. Everyone seems so utterly dedicated to figure skating – if they're not doing it, they're talking about it and if they're not talking about it or doing it, it's because they're asleep – and there just isn't time for anything else.

Better get my skates on (ho ho ho). I have a sesh with Madame von Berne in...ooooh! Now!

Frankie X

There was no time to lose. Hastily slinging her boot bag over her shoulder and nearly taking out the next computer, Frankie legged it from the IT room to the ice rink. She couldn't risk upsetting Madame, not in her first training session. Frankie needed to prove herself today. She needed to show the coaching director that she had what it took to be a champion.

She pushed open the double doors that led to

the ice rink and hurried inside, her steps slowing as the magnificence of the arena startled her again.

"Wow…" Frankie breathed, wondering if she'd ever get fed up with saying that. She looked for Madame. But apart from a boy and girl practising an overhead lift, the rink was empty.

Frankie laced up her boots at top speed. Then, deciding that it might be prudent to squeeze in a spot of last-minute practice before her tutor arrived, she stepped onto the ice. She began with some gentle stroking, working up to crossovers and then a slow camel spin.

"I see you've started without me."

The words were frosty.

Frankie's heart sank. She panicked. She pointed her toes inwards and came to a shuddering halt, silently cursing her total lack of grace. The snowplough stop was the most basic method of braking in the book. The method most favoured by five year olds.

"Sorry," she muttered, moving stiffly to the side.

The coaching director raised an eyebrow. "I

presume you've already warmed up?" she asked. It was obvious from her expression that she knew the answer.

Her heart plummeting yet further, Frankie shook her head. Now she was for it. She rarely did proper stretching. She knew it was important, but it seemed such a waste of time when she only had an hour on the ice. And the locals at Lee Valley would have laughed her out of the rink if they'd seen her bending and stretching like a piece of chewing gum. Her head drooped as she waited for the inevitable tongue-lashing.

"Make sure it doesn't happen again," the coaching director said mildly. "Perhaps you'd like to perform some leg stretches while I talk you through the ethos of the training school?"

It sounded like a question, but it was undeniably a command. Frankie didn't argue. Following Madame's instructions, she popped a foot on the barrier and stretched towards her toes. The coach took a seat and smoothed the wrinkles out of her sleek woollen dress. She folded her arms.

The woman meant business.

"First and foremost," began Madame von Berne, "you are here to win."

Frankie nodded. Actually, she was here to skate. She longed for Olympic gold, of course, but she'd seen how well Scarlett could skate and she didn't think there was room on the podium beside her for someone like Frankie. But she doubted if Madame would see it that way.

"Second, everyone else is here to win too. This is not a holiday camp for hobby skaters. It is not a safe haven for improving beginners. This is a prestigious training school, where skaters compete to be the best of the best before we unleash them on the rest of the world. Your fellow skaters are also your fiercest rivals. Do you understand?"

Frankie nodded again, more meekly now. She also swapped legs. If she'd stretched her left much more it would be longer than the right.

But Madame wasn't finished yet. "The school operates a fierce selection process," she added. "We encourage competition between students. It's excellent practice for real championships."

Alesha's cryptic comment was starting to make

sense. What had she told Frankie? That this wasn't the sort of place that encourages close friendships. So, was everyone encouraged to fight their way to the top at the expense of all else? Surely that couldn't actually be true...could it...? Well, Frankie reasoned, it would account for Alesha's weird comments and might, at a push, even begin to explain Scarlett's rather unconventional welcome.

"I see..." mumbled Frankie, not sure that she really saw at all. Even after the coach's explanation, it was all still deeply confusing to a girl who wasn't used to competing for anything more than possession of a netball. And she wasn't particularly good at that.

But the coach pounced on her words delightedly. "Marvellous," she replied. "Then we understand each other. Now, perhaps you'd like to run through some—" She broke off, with a look of comic-book horror. "No..." she said, half to herself. "That won't do at all."

"What?" whispered Frankie. By now, nothing would surprise her.

But Madame von Berne was apparently lost for

words. She pointed a trembling finger at Frankie's right foot, which was still balanced on the barrier. And then she spoke. "Take…it…off. Take *them* off. Now! Before your feet *shrivel*!"

It took Frankie a few seconds to work out that the coaching director was talking about her ice skates. Her precious figure-skating boots that she loved more than…well, she didn't love them more than life itself. But she certainly loved them more than Madame von Berne right now.

"*Off!*"

Frankie did as she was told.

Madame picked up one boot between her thumb and forefinger, and dangled it to and fro before her disgusted gaze. "And you've worn these for how long?" she asked.

"Nearly two years," whispered Frankie. "They were a present for my birth—"

"*Two years*," the coach interrupted. Minor details didn't appear to interest her. "I'm surprised you can walk, never mind skate." She held the skate at arm's length and released her pincer grip. The boot plummeted floorwards, bounced once and then laid still, its polished blade glinting uselessly.

"You won't be needing those any more," said Madame. She turned her attention to Frankie's stockinged feet. "I'll have our physio take a look at you to make sure no lasting damage has been done. You'll be fitted for new custom boots this afternoon, after lessons." She picked up her handbag – an ivory leather, quilted number with interlocking Cs – and prepared to leave.

Nervously, suddenly incomplete without her boots, Frankie clenched and unclenched her toes. Why she felt considerably more wibbly with her feet flat on the floor than she did balanced on two thin strips of metal was anyone's guess.

"Er…" she began.

The coaching director looked back.

"I was wondering what I should do now," mumbled Frankie, acutely aware of how silly she must sound, but also aware that as a capitalized New Girl, it wasn't unreasonable to expect a couple of pointers.

Madame von Berne's haughty expression thawed a couple of degrees and she smiled. "You're new," she said, as if she'd forgotten. "Breakfast is between seven and nine. And if you pop along to the secretary's office, she'll let you have everything else you need. Timetable, lesson plans, and so on." A small, brittle laugh escaped her. "I tend to forget about everyday interruptions, you see. For me, it's all about the skating. Nothing else really matters. It doesn't matter at all…" A faraway look appeared in her eyes. Was the coaching director remembering her own medal-winning hopes? Frankie had no way of knowing.

Then the shutters came down. In a split second, her dreamy gaze was replaced by the now familiar focused stare. "Of course, the very first thing you should do is find yourself a pair of shoes. We don't want to add chilblains to the potential problems of irresponsible boot-wear, do we?"

In a swirl of ivory knitted fabric, Madame von Berne left. The lesson was over.

CHAPTER *Ten*

Gripped by an irrational fear that Madame would whisk away her precious figure-skating boots and order them to be ceremonially burned, the first thing Frankie did was to hide them. Once they were squirrelled away in her suitcase, out of harm's way, she relaxed. And then, her stomach rumbling horribly, she remembered how hungry she was and decided to go for a late breakfast. Her timetable could wait. In the canteen, she found Alesha and Pippa and gratefully joined them for a hearty bowl of porridge.

After breakfast, Rosalie the secretary gave Frankie everything she needed to get through the school day. The timetable showed that there were lessons between 9 a.m. and 2 p.m., with a brief stop for lunch sandwiched in the middle. And then it was time for skating. Lots of it. Frankie took a deep breath. She was going to be very busy. So, as instructed by her timetable and following her plan of the school, she set off for her first lesson: English.

It wasn't so bad. Alesha had saved her a seat and the teacher was a kindly old man whose great passion in life was grammar. It was obvious that Mr. Douglas didn't give a monkey's that he was in the presence of future Olympic stars – a fact that didn't impress Scarlett Jones one bit.

"What's the point?" she complained loudly to Flic, when they were presented with a verb quiz. "Like I care whether it's a subjunctive or a past particle."

"Participle," muttered Flic, who set to with a biro.

"Whatever." Scarlett tutted. Then, when there

was no response from the other pupils, she scanned the room for allies.

"Miss Jones," said the English teacher tiredly, "if you want to stay behind for extra grammar practice, you are going the right way about it. I just hope it doesn't clash with skating…" He plucked a copy of *International Figure Skating* from his desk and casually began to leaf through the magazine.

Scarlett knew when she was beaten. In a flurry of exaggerated hair-flicking and eye-rolling, she turned her attention to the grammar quiz.

Frankie suppressed a giggle, thrilled beyond measure to see that the great Scarlett wasn't invincible.

The day got even better.

At lunchtime, Dylan beckoned her over to sit with him and his mates. "We can't let the new girl suffer the nutritionally balanced meal on her own, can we?" he said to the boys, who he went on to introduce as Paul and Woody.

Paul was small and wiry with dark hair. Woody was an unlikely-looking ice skater. He was solidly built and very tall, with curly blond hair and square-rimmed glasses. He clenched *New Scientist* in his left hand.

"Your five-a-day is something that shouldn't be attempted alone," Paul confirmed. "You need moral support to get you through it."

Woody stuck his fork into a pile of spinach. "Cover me," he groaned. "I'm going in."

With a grin, Frankie attacked her lasagne. It was decided. She might be missing her family and realizing that it might take a little longer until the Ice Palace felt like home, but right now, she was officially having A Good Time.

Physics was only half over when Frankie was summoned by the physio.

"Part-timer," muttered Scarlett as she left.

Frankie decided she wasn't going to let Scarlett's non-stop jibes bother her. She wasn't the one stuck with Newton and his pesky laws.

The physio was a slim woman called Ceri with sleek, dark hair and a mischievous glint in her eye. She nodded impatiently as Frankie explained how her old boots had been given their marching orders.

After a careful examination, Ceri pronounced the feet in question to be "absolutely fine", before fitting Frankie with moulded footbeds and sizing her up for new custom figure-skating boots. "Very narrow feet," she said. "Hmm." Abruptly, she yanked open a metal cupboard and selected a pair of white boots from the array stacked inside, before reaching for blades. "These should do nicely," she said. It took some time for Ceri to fit the blades onto the boots, but at last they were ready.

Frankie gazed in awe at the smooth, white leather and cool metal blades. They were just perfect.

She turned the brand-new boots over and over in her hands. Inside, they were lined with more stiff leather, with extra support around the ankle. She knew without whipping out a tape measure that the separate steel blades would be four millimetres wide, give or take a hair's breadth. It was something she often marvelled at – that it was possible to balance something as unwieldy as a person on them. She ran her fingers over the rough teeth at the front of the blades and then looked up at the physio with sparkling eyes.

They were the most beautiful boots she'd ever seen.

If her own boots were like old family friends – she knew them well and felt totally comfortable with them, despite what Madame might think – then these boots were like best mates. She felt as if she'd always had them. And they made her feel pretty fantastic too.

In short, they fitted a treat.

"Wow," she breathed.

"Go easy in them for a week or two," said Ceri. "The leather will be fairly stiff to start with."

Frankie nodded slowly, unable to drag her eyes from the magical ice skates.

The physio laughed. "Why don't you go and try them out?" she suggested. "You've half an hour before lessons finish. That should be long enough for a maiden voyage on the ice rink."

"Mmm…"

"That's unless you'd rather go back to physics?"

The spell was broken. Frankie thanked Ceri for her time and made for the door.

"Haven't you forgotten something?"

Frankie looked back, puzzled by the comment.

"Your boots will last a little longer if you save them for the ice," said the physio.

Pink-cheeked with embarrassment, Frankie clumped back to the squishy black patient's chair and changed into her trainers.

It was the third time she had skated at this rink. But it was the first time that Frankie had had the ice completely to herself.

This time, she made sure she warmed up properly, jogging on the spot until she was toasty. Then she did some slow stretches.

After shaking out her muscles, she finally launched herself away from the barrier, enjoying the freedom of such a large, empty space and the delicate crunch of metal on ice as she christened the new skates, stroking left…right…left…right.

Oooooh. The new boots were *good*.

She hummed Ravel's "Bolero" to herself as she glided across the ice, playing back Torvill and

Dean's Olympic-medal-winning dance in her head. Ice dancing wasn't her thing – she lacked a partner, for a start – but the world-famous routine was still one of her all-time favourites. Just a few notes of the rousing music was enough to remind her that she loved ice skating more than anything else in the world.

Growing used to the feel of the new footwear now, Frankie decided to attempt something more adventurous than stroking. How would the blades cope with a three-turn? There was only one way to find out.

The three-turn was named after the shape the skater's blade followed. When it was done well, a perfect figure "3" would remain behind, chiselled into the ice until more turns and twists scribbled it out. The turn was a basic one, but it took concentration to get it just right, and Frankie liked to think that hers wasn't bad.

She moved forward on her right foot, curving round to the left on an inside edge. So far, so good. At the pivotal moment, she bent her knee, pressed her blade forward and then swung backwards, her weight now transferred to the outside edge.

There was a smattering of applause…

…and the perfect day came to a grinding halt.

With horror, Frankie realized that she was no longer alone. Far from it. It appeared that every skater at the training centre was now gathered around the edge of the barrier, watching her performance. There were perhaps thirty of them.

And one of her.

"Come on, show us what you're made of, Frankie!" jeered Scarlett Jones. It was her – again! No matter how scary the others appeared, hanging over the barrier, they were just watching. Some of them were even smiling with encouragement. Scarlett was the only one actively being mean. "Lost your nerve?" she added. "Scared that we're better than you?"

There was a chorus of disapproval as Alesha, Dylan and the others tried to shout Scarlett down. But the girl would not be silenced.

"Not much of a performer, are you?" she sneered. "How are you going to cope in front of millions if you can't skate in front of us?"

The words were like missiles. Frankie skittered backwards to avoid them, felt herself lose her balance and then, with horrible inevitability, her new skates slid from beneath her and she landed on the ice with a thud.

"And that, my dear Olympic hopefuls," Scarlett announced gleefully, "is the gold-medal winner that we've heard so much about." She smiled broadly at the others. "Isn't she magnificent?"

"You're being unfair, Scarlett," muttered Dylan.

Frankie, who hadn't dared get up for fear of falling down again, kept her eyes firmly fixed on the ice. But she felt the tiniest glow of warmth at his words. Dylan had stood up for her. She had an ally! It was almost worth the tumble.

"She can't even fall with style," spluttered Scarlett, clearly unused to being challenged.

"On the contrary."

The voice was so cold and crisp that Frankie shivered. Still she didn't look up.

"Miss?" asked Scarlett, her voice bright and cheery now that the coaching director had appeared.

Frankie risked a glance and saw that the girl's glowering expression was gone and in its place was an innocent gaze.

Madame von Berne let the door clang shut behind her. "As you are all aware," she began, high heels clicking as she approached the barrier, "falling is an art."

Scarlett covered her mouth with perfectly manicured fingers. "Yeah, right," she coughed daintily.

"Even the most accomplished figure skaters fall," continued the coach. "And those who relax and go with gravity stand the least chance of being injured." She gestured towards the ice. "Here, you will have observed that Frankie executed a textbook fall. She slid to the side, thus avoiding her coccyx. I'm sure you all know how much *that* hurts."

There was a chorus of *ooh*s.

"Falling sideways also reduces the danger of hitting the skull on the ice, which can result in concussion and whiplash."

Everyone winced, even Scarlett. They'd all been there.

Madame von Berne continued. "Most importantly, Frankie did not use her hands to break her fall, something that can cause serious injury to the wrists. Hands up who'd like to shatter their radius and their ulna in one easy step." She scanned the crowd. "No takers? There are always the particularly nasty cases that require a titanium plate…"

By now, everyone was looking seriously uncomfortable. A few of the onlookers began to back away from the ice, muttering excuses about homework as they went. The rest sloped off to the far end of the rink to do their stretches.

In a matter of seconds, only Frankie and Madame remained.

Frankie scrambled to her feet and slid towards the barrier. In all her life, she'd never encountered such nastiness. This wasn't constructive criticism – it was totally personal. Scarlett Jones was out to get her. And Frankie had had enough.

Mustering all her courage, Frankie said the words that would solve everything. "Madame," she whispered, head down, "I want to go home."

The reply was swift, blunt and uncompromising. "Nonsense."

Frankie, who'd been expecting sympathy and softly spoken entreaties to stay, looked up in bewilderment. "But—"

"No buts," said Madame briskly. "You've been with Team GB for a little over twenty-four hours. I won't allow you to give up now." From her vantage point behind the barrier, the petite woman was able to look Frankie right in the eyes. Her sapphire-blue irises were chilly with disapproval.

"If figure skating were easy," she said, her voice rimed with frost, "everyone would do it. But it isn't easy. It's a demanding sport that requires every last bit of determination that you can give." She pursed her lips. "Scarlett Jones is just one of the obstacles that you will have to overcome if you want to do well. You can listen to her and believe her and let her comments wear you down. Or" – here she paused meaningfully – "you can ignore her and concentrate on beating her instead." The coach raised her eyebrows. "Well?" she demanded. "What's it to be?"

Frankie gulped. She loved skating so, so much. But was it worth the grief that Scarlett seemed compelled to dish out at every opportunity? Was it worth the effort and endless practice that her new timetable promised? Was it worth living away from her family?

Was it?

It was.

"Yes," she said quietly. "I'd like to stay."

There was no trumpeting fanfare to celebrate her announcement, just a small satisfied nod from Madame von Berne. "Good," she said, her forehead relaxing as if an iron had smoothed out the worried wrinkles. "Now, how are those boots? Better?"

CHAPTER *Eleven*

Frankie had rather hoped the bedroom would be empty, but they were all there when she got back from the rink. Scarlett was lounging in the only armchair, idly flicking through a magazine, while Flic was huddled on her bunk, wearing a nervous expression. Alesha rolled her eyes in Scarlett's direction and Frankie got the message.

She was in for it.

Scarlett's attack wasn't long in coming. "Were today's flights fully booked?" she said, ominously offhand.

Frankie shook her head. She shut the door behind her, pulled open her bedside drawer and rummaged inside, eventually locating her lime-green iPod – quite possibly the best Christmas present ever – among the debris. Nonchalantly, she ran her finger over its smooth surface as she chose a song.

"Then how come you're still here?" Scarlett went on. "You must know that I've always been the best skater around here. Why are you even bothering to compete? It seems like the only thing you can do properly is fall."

"Huh?" Frankie could sense that the other girl was becoming annoyed by her lack of response. She'd worked out why Scarlett was being so mean to her. The girl didn't want to lose her crown as Queen of the Ice. Because she was good – dazzling, even. Anyone could see that. Only Frankie had suddenly realized that she wanted to be better.

"When. Are. You. Going. Home?"

The words were like punches, but Frankie didn't flinch. "I'm not," she said quietly.

Scarlett laughed. "I don't think you heard me

right," she said in a dangerously low voice. "I asked when you were going home."

"Oh, I heard you perfectly well," replied Frankie, holding her nerve. "And I'm not. Going home, that is. At least, not until the British Junior Championships in London."

The other girl's face was puce with anger. It clashed horribly with her tracksuit. "But—" she spluttered.

"But what?" interrupted Frankie. She was feeling braver now, especially after catching a glimpse of Alesha's thrilled face. Flic just looked stunned, but Frankie knew that she'd receive no support from her – the girl was a fully paid-up member of Team Velour. Quickly she continued, before she wimped out of her speech. "Why should I stay when you've done your best to make me feel unwelcome?" she asked. "Is that what you want to know? Why haven't I been put off by your scare tactics?" She looked Scarlett right in the eyes, trying not to flinch from the sparks of anger that flew from them.

Scarlett said nothing. She didn't need to.

"Because you're not worth it," Frankie said, feeling a huge rush of adrenalin as she forced out the words. At the same time, she felt very odd. This wasn't the real Frankie. She didn't act like this. The Frankie she'd always known – and rather liked – didn't have stand-up rows with anyone other than her brother, and certainly not with someone as prickly as Scarlett. It was by far the bravest thing she'd ever done. But deep down, she knew that if she wanted to survive at the Ice Palace, it was the only thing *to* do.

"No one speaks to me like that," said Scarlett. The fluffy teddy she'd been idly stroking was now being quietly throttled in her clenched fist.

"I just did," Frankie said softly. Then, partly because she was too soft-centred to keep up the tough-girl exterior and partly because she was beginning to wilt, just a little bit, beneath Scarlett's white-hot gaze, she relented and gave a placatory smile. "Why don't we save our arguments for the ice?" she suggested. "If you're as good as you say you are, then you've no reason to worry. You'll still be the star."

The words didn't have the calming effect that Frankie had hoped for. If anything, Scarlett looked even angrier than before. She'd raked agitated fingers through her long blonde mane so many times that it now resembled a messy bale of straw.

"Sounds fair enough to me," said Alesha.

There was an awkward silence. Flic glanced nervously between Scarlett and Frankie, clearly not daring to say a word, while Alesha simply beamed with undisguised joy.

"Fine," snapped Scarlett.

And that was it. With a curious sense of anticlimax, the argument was over.

Scarlett flung her teddy onto her make-up strewn duvet and flounced from the room. Flic slithered down from her bunk and scampered after her. In the distance, she could be heard making soothing comments, before Scarlett shrieked, "Shut up!"

Frankie felt a sudden urge to giggle. And before she knew what was happening, she was howling with laughter, great peals of it building up inside her before bursting out and ringing around the dorm.

Alesha smiled happily. "Well done," she said, giving Frankie's hand a firm shake. "Hey, if your ice skating is half as good as your talent for putting Miss Smarty Pants in her place, you'll go far."

Frankie nodded helplessly. In a way, she didn't care if Scarlett were the better skater. The challenge was simply a means of shutting the other girl up – for now. Then perhaps she'd get the chance to do what she'd come here for, without the interruptions that were driving her crazy.

She was going to learn to skate. And she was going to do it properly.

"Come on," said Alesha, beckoning from the doorway. "After a speech like that, I think you deserve a dodgy cappuccino from the machine in the common room."

Frankie grinned. "Do you know what?" she replied. "I think I do!"

CHAPTER *Twelve*

Frankie's one-to-one figure-skating lessons started in earnest the very next morning. It seemed that Madame Kristiana von Berne was as impatient as her to get started, as she'd arranged for them to meet on the ice at 6.30 a.m., long before most people were awake, never mind up, dressed and laced into brand-new, slightly stiff figure skates. A few skaters zoomed around the ice, but there was plenty of room left for Frankie.

Madame arrived at 6.30 on the dot. The horribly

early hour was no obstacle to the coach's pristine appearance. As usual, she was coordinated and accessorized like a *Vogue* model, with make-up so flawless it might have been Photoshopped. Frankie found herself wondering if it were normal to be so perfect all the time, but Madame's curt comment cut short her ponderings.

"We'll start with stopping," said the coaching director. "You need to learn how to stop properly before you can move with anything approaching confidence," said Madame, with impeccable logic.

Frankie nodded. She couldn't argue with that. A shiver of excitement ran through her. Now was her chance to show the coach what she was really made of. It she did well, maybe they *would* move on to spins by breakfast. She glided forward on one foot before coming to a neat T-stop.

"No, no, no, *not* like that…"

In utter amazement, Frankie slowly lowered her outstretched arms until they hung limply at her sides. Couldn't she even get the basic T-stop right? This was going to be harder than she'd thought.

"Again," said the coach. "And this time slowly…

more gracefully. The T-stop is *not* the way to stop if you're in a hurry. It is controlled and beautiful. As you stop, your skates should form a perfect T. The back foot is the horizontal part of the T and the front foot is the vertical." She punctuated her advice with a sharp clap. "Again!"

Frankie did it again. And again. And again and again and again until she might have screamed with frustration, had she not been so totally mad about skating. So she glided forward on her right foot, bringing the left lightly towards it, increasing the pressure to slow herself down. Then she repeated the move, gliding on her left foot this time. Then her right. Left. Right. Over and over she glided and stopped until her legs were trembling like a jelly on a wobbly table.

Every step, edge, posture, movement, *everything* had to be unlearned and relearned, with added polish. And once Frankie swallowed her disappointment that she wouldn't be progressing to Biellmann spins anytime soon, she found that she was enjoying herself. *Really* enjoying herself. It was one thing to teach yourself, copying the moves that you'd seen on the small screen and practising them until you were pretty sure they were okay, but it was quite another to be briskly informed by an expert that something was "shocking" or "with a little more lift here and a touch more extension there, it would be *so* much better". For once, she didn't need to guess if she was doing it properly. She *knew*. No one had ever taken such an interest in her skating before and it felt great.

At last, when Frankie was sure that there would be enough time to establish a space colony on the moon before she cracked it, Madame nodded with approval. "Good," she said.

Her exhausted pupil grinned widely. She felt like treating herself to a lap of honour and whooping with joy. But there was no room in Madame's timetable for unnecessary celebration.

The coach glanced at her watch. "We've just time to look at the basics of stroking," she announced.

Frankie giggled. She couldn't help it. She knew that it was proper figure-skating terminology, but it sounded so *silly*. Stroking always brought to mind cats and dogs and hamsters, not the smooth movement of blade on ice.

Madame shook her head. "Every single time…" she muttered under her breath. Then she clapped her hands again and, with barely time to glug a quenching mouthful of water, off Frankie went.

After the staccato practice of stopping techniques, it was a release to be performing fluid moves, where Frankie could really pick up some speed. But Madame's stern clap brought her to a perfectly executed T-stop. Again. She sighed. She was *loving* the skating, but she did think they were going to progress a little faster than this. When were they going to get on to the dazzling jumps, the dizzying spins…?

Madame seemed to recognize Frankie's impatience and she dealt with it swiftly. "I hardly need remind you that good stroking skills are *imperative* if you are to skate like a champion," she barked. She marched around the perimeter of the rink to where Frankie stood nervously. "Tell me," she said, "why do *you* think that it is important to stroke well?"

"I…er…" At the sudden question, Frankie's mouth went horribly dry. She knew the answer to this, she really did. Unfortunately, her memory had chosen this precise moment to take a holiday. "To g-g-get across the ice?" she stammered.

"To get across the ice," repeated Madame von Berne slowly. "Well, that's one way of looking at it, I suppose." She took a deep breath.

Instinctively, Frankie gripped the barrier, steadying herself against the torrent of angry words that she was certain was heading her way. She'd really done it now. The coach would be furious at her lame explanation.

But when it came, Madame's reply was strangely subdued. She spoke softly, staring glassy-eyed at goodness-knows-what. "Stroking allows a skater to perform controlled entrances and exits, to skate smoothly and beautifully…" Her words petered out as she gazed into the distance. She might have been here in body, but her mind was definitely elsewhere.

Frankie shivered. This was a little unnerving. But, as suddenly as she'd gone into the odd trance,

Madame snapped out of it. "On a very basic level, stroking is the glue that sticks a successful routine together," she said curtly, her blue eyes focused and steady. There was no trace of the softer, more vulnerable woman who'd taken her place. "Now, try again. And this time, do it properly."

"It was totally weird," Frankie told Alesha after breakfast, as they oohed and aahed over impossible-looking jumps in the entrance-hall gallery.

"Uh-huh." Alesha nodded slowly. "And you say that she didn't seem herself?" she asked, in a manner so like a TV detective that Frankie half-expected her to flip out a notebook and start making notes.

"Not at all," she replied. "It was like she was on another planet or had been taken over by aliens. Very knowledgeable aliens, but aliens all the same." She frowned, thinking back to how Madame had drifted off. Afterwards, the coach had been abrupt, humourless and stern. So, back to her normal self. "Do you think she was remembering how she skated before her accident?" she mused.

Alesha frowned and pursed her lips theatrically, before eventually admitting, "Dunno." She shrugged. "She doesn't give much away, our wonderful coach. Keeps herself to herself. She'd be rubbish on a chat show."

Frankie couldn't help laughing.

"Anyway…" Alesha folded her arms and rocked back on her heels, grinning widely. "How do you feel after your chat with Scarlett last night? There aren't many people who've stood up to her, you know."

"Really?" Last night, Frankie had felt as fearless and invincible as a comic-book hero, but in the cold light of a Swiss autumn day, she was wondering if perhaps she'd gone over the top. It might not have been the best idea to antagonize the Queen of the Ice Palace. Because however much it annoyed Frankie, Scarlett really was a terrific skater – when she stopped being mean long enough to skate, that was. And what if her comments had just made Scarlett more determined to destroy the opposition? "Yeah, well…I, er…thought it was better to…stand up for myself." Quickly, she tried to change the subject, but Alesha was having none of it.

"Just for the record, I thought you were fab," she said. "Scarlett's had that coming to her for ages." Alesha grinned, showing that when she relaxed her habitually fed-up expression, she really was very pretty. "A few of us are going to watch repeats of last year's World Figure Skating Championships in the common room," she said. "Just as a little light relief before this afternoon's group skating session. Fancy it?"

Did she fancy it? *Was an ice rink slippery?* Frankie nodded eagerly.

She was slowly starting to feel as if she fitted in here. And, if she wasn't very much mistaken – and in spite of the dire warnings doled out by Alesha herself that friendships weren't allowed – Frankie thought that she might have made her very first proper friend in Switzerland.

Chapter *Thirteen*

To: mumndadnjoshnjessnmeg
From: Frankieonthemove
Subject: Coffee cakes rule!

Dear Mum and everyone else, but especially
Mum, who bakes THE best cakes,

Thank you! It was THE most delicious thing
I ever tasted in my life. Seriously. Better than
chicken jalfrezi.

I miss you all loads – even you, Josh – but

I'm learning so much stuff it's untrue. Madame's giving me one-to-one lessons every morning. That's on top of the daily skating practice, not to mention the schoolwork – bleurgh.

One week down, seven to go. I'll be back before you know it.

Hugs and kisses,

Frankie X

In no time at all, life at the Ice Palace had settled into a comfortable and familiar rhythm. Frankie discovered that Alesha had a wicked sense of humour that never failed to make her chuckle. And although Frankie e-mailed Rosie every week, it was so nice to have another friend who loved skating as much as she did.

Frankie had made friends with a couple of the other girls too. Pippa was one of the older ones. She was a sweet-natured girl with cropped blonde hair and dark brown eyes, who always had time to explain the ins and outs of Ice Palace life to its newest recruit. Pippa had an uncanny knack of sensing which day curry would be on the menu and making sure that she and Frankie got to the canteen before it was all eaten. And her spins were pretty cool too.

Meanwhile, Frankie was practising very hard. Sunday, Monday, Tuesday, Wednesday…no matter what day it was, her alarm dragged her out of bed while it was still dark. And at 6.30 a.m. precisely, she braved Madame von Berne at the ice rink.

The coach was tireless in her pursuit of the perfect hockey stop, the perfect sculling technique, the perfect forward glide… The list went on. But slowly, sometimes so slowly that she felt as if she were going backwards, Frankie gradually began to lose her old, sloppy habits. It wasn't that Madame heaped oodles of praise on her – the most Frankie ever got was a curt "good" – but the criticisms became less stinging. Even though they still hadn't embarked on anything as ambitious as a routine, the coach had promised that once she was satisfied with her newest pupil's edges, they would.

Frankie could hardly wait.

On weekdays, the mornings were crammed with

schoolwork. Maths, English, languages, science, art... Frankie idly contemplated that if scientists would only hurry up with their cloning research, she could order a carbon copy of herself. It would make it so much easier to get everything done.

After lessons finished at 2 p.m., Frankie joined the group training sessions with Mr. Pearson, who everyone called by his first name, Rob. First, the students would warm up. Then, they would perform a few basic moves – trying to keep in perfect time with each other – before moving on to the day's "Star Move" as Rob called it. It might be a difficult jump or a spin or something quite everyday like an outside spread eagle. Each pupil tried to make the Star Move as perfect as possible and then the coach would incorporate the move into a short, choreographed sequence, which they all practised. The lesson finished with a short performance from each of them. Afterwards, they were all asked to give constructive criticism or praise and Frankie found that the opinions of her fellow students were just as valid as the coach's comments. Frankie proved to be an incredibly fast learner. And although her jumps didn't always come off, when they did, they were spectacular. The feeling was indescribable… It was huge fun.

Frankie was in the same group as Alesha, which was great. (And she was in a different group to Scarlett, which was even better.) The lessons gave her the opportunity to check out some of the others' skating. Frankie's jaw dropped when she saw Alesha on the ice. She had seen her skate before, but she hadn't realized that she was such a daredevil. Her jumps dazzled, but were tinged with danger too. Frankie found that she held her breath whenever Alesha leaped from the ice – anxious that her new friend would come safely back down to earth – and then sighed with relief when she landed again.

Watching Alesha might be scary, but it was anything but boring.

On the days that Ally Williams was in charge of the group sessions, she concentrated on posture. "You can jump as high as you like," the coach said, "but if you're too stiff or too floppy or if your elbows are sticking out like a pantomime chicken, then you're *never* going to win."

Three times a week, they had gym. Frankie hadn't grasped just how important fitness was until she encountered the aptly named Miss Panter and her punishing regime of circuits, circuits and yet more circuits. The gym teacher assessed Frankie's fitness level as "average" and her flexibility as "stiffer than a fillet of frozen cod", but she was impressed with her core strength. Frankie was given her own list of exercises to perform during the endless laps of the gym. These exercises would help her all-round fitness and improve her stamina, which was vital if she were to last the three and a half *looooong* minutes of the freestyle programme. Extra stretches would help with the general bendiness that she lacked.

On the days that they didn't hurl themselves around the gym, the students were back on the ice for one-to-one tuition or extra practice.

Finally, there was just enough time to gobble down tea before the evening's free skate and for them to squeeze in homework before bed.

It was utterly exhausting.

But it was utterly brilliant.

* * *

Meanwhile, Scarlett kept a low profile. The Queen of the Ice restricted herself to furious glares and muttered asides about it being compulsory for learner skaters to wear L-plates, but that was all. Whenever she and Frankie shared the ice, she kept to the other end of the rink, flanked by Flic and Bethany, her faithful sidekicks. At bedtime, Scarlett simply ignored the new girl.

Frankie had even managed to get over her blushes when talking to Lovely Dylan. He was still lovely – and very good at warning her when something on the canteen menu was totally inedible – but what with the early mornings and the even earlier nights, coupled with a learning curve as steep as the Eiger, Frankie told herself firmly that she didn't have time for a silly crush. No, she really didn't.

She missed her family horribly. Even though she managed to make it to the IT room to e-mail them once a day, it wasn't nearly enough. The home-made coffee cake that Mum sent at the end of the first week was a masterpiece of sponge, squidgy filling, shiny icing and walnuts. And it had made her feel *so* homesick. But as the days went by and she made it to the end of week two, Frankie discovered that she was able to bear the distance between herself and London just that bit easier. Thinking of her family now made her smile wistfully instead of sob. It was only six weeks until she'd be going back. And she was *loving* the skating. Everything was settling down rather nicely…

…until Madame dropped her bombshell.

"Did you *hear*?" Scarlett announced to Flic and, apparently, the rest of Switzerland, so loud was her voice.

Frankie couldn't help listening in. She would've had to have been deaf not to.

"Huh?" Flic looked up vacantly, a spoon brimming with cereal and milk suspended midway between bowl and mouth.

"Trials," said Scarlett. She gave a conspiratorial wink.

"Huh?" repeated Flic.

That was all the excuse Scarlett needed. Expertly swiping a golden curtain of hair behind one ear, she leaned forward to address her subjects. Flic and Bethany mirrored her movements, breakfast forgotten in the face of this intrigue.

Scarlett took a deep breath before beginning. "Madame von Berne—"

"—will be making her own announcements," interrupted the woman herself. "Thank you, Scarlett."

Scarlett had the decency to blush, while everyone else tried not to giggle.

The coach calmly helped herself to muesli and fruit before taking a seat at the teachers' table, seemingly oblivious to the hush that had settled on the canteen and the expectant looks that everyone now wore.

Frankie was just as fascinated as the rest of them. She might have spent another gruelling hour and a half with Madame at the rink that morning, but that didn't mean she'd been privy to the coach's thoughts. Mechanically, she fed mouthful after mouthful of soggy Weetabix into her mouth, while keeping her eyes firmly fixed on Madame von Berne.

There wasn't a peep from Scarlett, who was doing her level best to look unrepentant and smug, but not really pulling it off.

After five silent minutes, the coach took pity on them all. "I will explain everything fully in the gym at 9 a.m.," she said. "But if anyone can't wait that long, you'll find details pinned to the noticeboard in the common room."

It appeared that *no one* could wait that long. In seconds, all the students had decamped to the common room, where curiosity had reached fever pitch. Marianne read the notice aloud.

"*The British Junior Championships take place in six weeks' time. All those under nineteen are eligible to take part, but must satisfy certain criteria before they are allowed to do so. In order that we may assess your routines, trials will be held in three weeks' time. Anyone who does not achieve the required standard will not be competing in the Championships and their status at the training centre will be reviewed.*"

"Oh, is that *all*?" said Marianne, with a hefty sigh. "I thought it was something *important*."

"*What do you mean?*" shrieked Scarlett, who was

having considerable trouble staying below the safe limit for decibels this morning. "It's important to *me*!"

Marianne grinned apologetically. "Sorry, hon," she said, patting her on the shoulder. "I thought it was something to do with the Winter Olympics. I know it means the world to you, but I'm nineteen. Doesn't apply."

Others nodded and, one by one, drifted away from the noticeboard until just nine students remained. Frankie was one of them. At just fourteen, she was among the very youngest. There was Scarlett, obviously. And Flic and Bethany. Dylan, Woody and Paul were there too, as well as Milly Black, a quiet girl who just last week had done her first triple toe-loop. Alesha stood at the back, looking as if she'd lost a tenner and found ten pence. Her dark features were etched with misery.

Frankie was confused. Why did Alesha look so glum? Was she worried about the trials? She flung an arm round Alesha's shoulder. "What's up?" she said softly.

Alesha sniffed. "Sorry, got to go." She shrugged off Frankie's arm and fled from the common room as if the paparazzi were chasing her.

"Ha!" Flic laughed shortly. "I might have known this would freak her out." She smiled as Alesha charged past the common room window. She cut a forlorn figure – hood up, head down, hands firmly wedged in her pockets.

Scarlett's angry expression had quickly switched to one of triumph. "One less for us to worry about, eh?" she crowed. "There's no way she'll make it through the trials. Not after last time. Alesha might be a good skater, but she just can't cope with pressure." And she laughed loudly.

Frankie didn't have to listen to this. But she did need to find out what was going on.

She went after her friend.

CHAPTER *Fourteen*

Frankie had been sure that Alesha would retreat to the dorm, but she hadn't. She wasn't in the IT room either. On a whim, Frankie checked the locker room, but it was deserted. Just as she was about to leave though, she noticed that a locker door gaped open, empty save for a pair of scuffed Doc Marten's.

There was only one person at the Ice Palace who wore those.

Quickly, Frankie hurried down the alleyway of

lockers and nudged open the swing doors to the ice rink.

There, in the middle of the ice, a solitary figure was angrily flinging herself about, with scant regard for safety or style.

"Alesha!" cried Frankie, running to the barrier.

Either the girl didn't hear her or she was lost in a world of her own. Frankie could only watch the display with a mixture of awe and fear. She'd never seen anyone ice-skate like this before, not even Alesha herself, whose moves were always verging on reckless.

Alesha performed a stylish three-turn, exiting on a left outside edge with her arms and free leg extended behind her body and her skating knee bent. Then she took off, spinning and then landing with incredible precision on her right skate. Frankie hardly recognized it as an Axel jump. Gone were the smooth, graceful lines and in their place was a swift, angry leap.

Releasing the breath that she'd unconsciously held while Alesha was airborne, Frankie barely had time to take another before her friend swooped round to the left again, now turning backwards. She swung her right foot round in an arc before leaving the ice, rotating twice and landing backwards on the right foot. Whereas the Axel jump had one-and-a-half rotations, the daring double Salchow had two full revolutions – 720 amazing degrees of spin.

"Wow!"

The spell was broken. Alesha looked up in surprise, dug in a toe pick and promptly overbalanced, landing with an "Oof!" on the ice.

Frankie rushed forward as quickly as someone wearing trainers could navigate slippery ice. She remained upright – just – but by the time she'd slithered and slid towards her friend, Alesha was hugging her knees tightly and rocking gently to and fro. Sobs shook her narrow shoulders.

"Are you okay?" Frankie gasped, landing in an ungainly heap beside her friend.

"*No-oh-oh-oh*," wailed Alesha.

Frankie cautiously touched her friend's shoulder. "What is it?" she asked softly. "Can I help?"

"N-n-not unless you can teach me how to skate before the trials." Alesha gave a huge, noisy sniff and looked up, revealing a blotchy face, streaked with tears.

Frankie was totally confused. "What do you *mean*?" she said. She'd just watched Alesha perform two tricky jumps in quick succession. And what the jumps lacked in finesse, they more than made up for with sheer nerve. "I've just seen you skate like a champion!" she exclaimed. "You're much better than me."

"Yeah, right," mumbled Alesha, but she was quieter now.

"Why don't you tell me what's wrong?" said Frankie. "Come on, before we get frostbitten bottoms." She smiled as she got unsteadily to her feet and hauled her friend upright too. "And that's not an easy thing to say, never mind treat."

Despite herself, Alesha giggled.

"Tow me to the kiss-and-cry area," suggested Frankie. "No one will disturb us there. You can tell me all about it."

Pulling Frankie along behind her, Alesha headed for the small, enclosed space at the far end of the rink. Because it was sometimes used for competitions, this rink was modelled on a championship venue. The kiss-and-cry area was where figure skaters bit their nails and waited nervously for their scores to be announced. There were wooden seats set against a backdrop of a Swiss tourism poster, just in case there were film crews and journalists there to record the delighted or resolutely brave faces of the figure skaters as they discovered whether they'd won or lost. Would it be kisses of victory or disappointed sobs…?

Bit by bit, Frankie managed to winkle the whole sorry tale out of Alesha. She and Scarlett went back a long way, it seemed. They'd both been talented-spotted by Madame's spies at Alexandra Palace in London. Not that they'd trained together. Scarlett had had intensive one-to-one tuition with a former medal-winner, while Alesha had travelled in from Swindon every weekend for elite group lessons.

Two shaky signatures on dotted lines later, they arrived a year ago on the same plane from Heathrow. They might have been friends, if Scarlett hadn't travelled first class. And Alesha was so shy that she had difficulty making friends with someone in the next airline seat, never mind someone on the other side of the posh curtain.

"I adore the skating…" said Alesha, tears welling up again. "If I'm alone on the ice, it's great. Make me compete and I crumble quicker than a sandcastle in an earthquake. I thought I'd get used to it, but I just can't stand the pressure. I may as well go home, you know. There's no way I'd be able to cope at the Olympics."

"But you don't know that," said Frankie reasonably.

"I do," sobbed Alesha. "Ever since the end-of-term competition, I've been hopeless… My confidence is shot to bits."

Alesha explained. In July, Madame had held a small competition. Nothing flash, just a free skate to get the students used to competing. Alesha had worked with Madame to create a wonderfully daring routine, which she would perform to the tune of her favourite Madonna song. It had to be an instrumental version of course – lyrics weren't allowed in the music. There were loops, Axels,

Salchows and, to finish, a death-drop spin.

"What happened?" asked Frankie. She didn't need to be psychic to know that this story wasn't going to have a happy ending.

"I tripped up getting onto the ice," muttered Alesha. "Ended up skidding across the ice on my behind before I'd even started." She blushed. "But then I tried, I really did. You know how Madame tells us that even if we make a mistake in the first five seconds, we've to carry on regardless? Give it our best shot?"

Frankie nodded encouragingly.

"I couldn't have skated any worse if they'd blindfolded me and tied my legs together. The death-drop spin was the worst bit of all. I landed on my face."

"Oh."

"Scarlett's never let me forget it."

"I see."

Frankie did see. It all became clear now – why Alesha was a bit of a loner, why Scarlett made cruel jokes and why her confidence had now hit rock bottom.

Alesha took a deep breath and struggled wearily to her feet. She turned to face Frankie, her eyes accusing. "You wouldn't understand what it's like to be scared," she said angrily. "You've got nothing to worry about. You're a natural, everyone says so. You'll have to put the hours in, of course you will. But you'll get there. It's different for me. I have to *really* work at it. And if I don't do well in these trials, I'll be on the first plane home."

She stumbled away from the kiss-and-cry area and onto the rink. As she skated away, the sound of blade on ice was as harsh as her words.

CHAPTER *Fifteen*

Suddenly, everything was deadly serious.

Where before, there had been room for the odd joke…

"What do you call a figure skater with an ice-cream cone in each ear?"

"Anything you like – they can't hear you!"

…now, the nine students under the magic age of nineteen were concentrating wholeheartedly on choreographing their routines. In turn, each of them visited Madame to discuss their ideas, Frankie included. Finally she was being allowed to move on from the basics.

Scarlett told anyone who would listen that she couldn't decide whether to go for a double Lutz or go straight for the triple. "Yes, definitely the triple," she decided at full volume in the canteen.

"Yeah, right," muttered Paul under his breath. "And I'll be throwing in a flip-loop-loop combo, of course. That's before I spin on my head."

Frankie grinned. She couldn't help feeling excited about the trials, but she had just three weeks to perfect a two-minute routine that had to include at least three jumps, three spins and two fast-step sequences – and Madame hadn't allowed her to do anything more complicated than a Salchow yet. If she thought about it too much, it became *really* scary. She *so* didn't want to be sent home without even a chance to compete in the British Junior Championships. She didn't want her Olympic dream to end *now*. To distract herself, she tried to cheer up Alesha. But if anything, that was even trickier than working on her first routine.

Alesha was now seriously demotivated. She was

operating on a need-to-speak basis. If she didn't need to speak, she didn't. No matter how hard Frankie tried to coax her into a normal conversation, Alesha cut her short with a shake of the head – or simply ignored her. It was impossible to penetrate the wall of silence.

Not even Scarlett's jibes could elicit a response. "Will you be doing a death-drop this time?" she asked in a treacly voice. "It was so good last time. *Soooo* realistic."

"Just ignore her," said Frankie.

But Alesha did better than that. She ignored *both* of them. If they'd been dishing out medals for sheer stubbornness, she would have been on top of the podium, no question.

While she was figuring out how to get through to Alesha, Frankie concentrated on her skating technique. Her daily lessons with Madame had now covered inside and outside spread eagles, so called because of the spreadeagled position of her body and the fact that the skater faced either the inside or outside of the circle as they curved round. Secretly, Frankie called them her Mary Poppins moves, because of the turned-out position of her feet, but she didn't share the nickname with Madame for the simple reason that she didn't truly believe the coach had a sense of humour. She certainly never displayed any evidence of one. And no one at the Ice Palace was brave enough to crack a joke to test the theory.

But whatever Madame lacked in basic comedy skills, she more than made up for with truly inspired teaching methods. During the very next week, she considered that Frankie had improved to such an extent that it was time for spins.

Spins!

Frankie *adored* spins. *Really* adored them. Spinning on the spot, so fast that the world became a colourful, meaningless blur, was one of the most thrilling things about figure skating. She loved the combination of total control – the moment a skater lost their concentration during a spin was the moment it all went horribly wrong – and the sheer joy of giving herself up completely to the ice.

One dark, chilly October morning, the spinning began in earnest.

"Show me what you can do."

Madame's tone was even more clipped than usual. She planted a mohair-clad elbow on the barrier and propped her dainty chin on her hand to watch as Frankie skated tentatively onto the ice. This morning, she was gripped with a fierce determination to succeed. She was fed up with "Do this, not that" and "Again". No, she wanted "Wow!" and "Bravo!" Frankie was going to show Madame the best forward sit spin ever. Or crash trying.

Last week, she'd practised the hilariously named shoot-the-duck until her gluteus maximus muscles – basically, the muscles she sat on – were screaming out for mercy. The shoot-the-duck was simply a forward sit spin without the spin. Gliding forward on one leg, Frankie bent her skating knee with the other leg stretched straight out in front... She didn't regard it as the most glamorous movement in *The Big Book of Figure Skating*, but add rotation and suddenly it became a whole lot more stylish.

As with most spins, the forward sit spin began with back crossovers. Frankie reversed smoothly around the edge of the rink, simultaneously building up speed and courage. When she felt ready, she held a right inside edge while swinging round her left leg, transferring her weight to her left foot and bending low. A three-turn hooked the spin and she swung out her right leg until it was parallel with the ice, and she was spinning anticlockwise. Frankie leaned forwards with her hands lightly crossed. Gleefully clocking the fact that she'd got into position without sitting down on the ice, she gave herself up to the spin.

Wheeeeeeeeeeeeee! she thought, because to say it aloud would have been the polar opposite of cool.

After weeks of going back to boring old basics, it was such a relief to revel in the pure enjoyment of a spin for a few seconds. Feeling her speed decreasing, she prepared to exit the move. She leaned forward, bringing round her right leg and straightening the left until she was upright.

Phew! She'd done it.

There was an ominous silence.

Not daring to look up, Frankie cautiously skated to the edge of the rink, resisting the urge to hook a skate behind her and squeeze in a pull-up spin.

With a gentle swoosh, she came to a halt beside the barrier. Mustering all her courage, she looked up. And then, because she was quite sure that she must be seeing things, she did a double take.

Madame was smiling. Not the lopsided smile that accompanied her most stinging criticisms, but a real, true-life smile. With teeth and everything.

"Excellent," said the coach.

It wasn't the "Wow" or "Bravo" that Frankie had dreamed of, but it meant everything to her. "Really?" she breathed.

"Really," said Madame Kristiana von Berne.

It felt to Frankie just as if she had cool, sparkling lemonade running through her veins. The shivery tingle extended to her fingertips and her toes and the tip of her nose until she was fizzing all over with excitement. She'd done it. She'd impressed Madame at last!

Woooooooooooooooooooooo!

But the coach didn't whoop with joy. Her eyes had a faraway, unfocused look that meant that she was in a world of her own again.

"A very long time ago," began the coach, so softly

that her pupil had to strain to hear the words, "I was like you. A natural, they all said. Bound to go far… And I did, you know. As far as the World Championships."

Frankie felt as if she were eavesdropping. And, like an eavesdropper, she knew that she couldn't betray her presence for fear of stopping Madame mid-flow.

"I lost my concentration, you see. That was my downfall. I should have been focusing on my performance, but foolishly, I was thinking of…" Her voice tailed off.

By now, Frankie was almost dancing on her toe picks, so great was her curiosity. What had the coach been thinking of that was so distracting it made her trip and lose her footing – and the gold medal with it? It had to be something totally romantic. Unrequited love, that must be it! "Yes?" she prompted impatiently, forgetting her vow to remain silent.

The mood changed instantly.

"*What?*" snapped Madame. *Pouf!* The whimsical gaze vanished.

Cautiously, Frankie tried to lure her back into

storytelling mode. "You were telling me—"

"I was telling you that your forward sit spin was passable," said the coach briskly. "And if you have quite finished wasting my time, I suggest we proceed to the back sit spin. Begin from a back outside edge, please."

Frankie nodded. She accelerated towards the centre of the ice, before pivoting and starting the back crossovers. When Madame was in one of *those* moods, obedience was the only option. But she had been given a tantalizing glimpse into the closed book that was Madame Kristiana von Berne's past. She wasn't just the best-dressed trainer in Switzerland. There was emotion beneath that cool, sleek exterior, and a mysterious past too. And Frankie was going to find out all about it.

After she'd wowed the coach with her back sit spin, of course.

CHAPTER *Sixteen*

"Girls?" trilled Scarlett from her top bunk. "Do you think I'd look better in pink satin with silver sequins or lilac silk with a sparkly netting trim?"

There was no respite from the build-up to the trials, not even after bedtime. Frankie tried to drown out Felicity's simpering response by boosting the volume on her iPod, but a well-aimed fluffy teddy knocked out her earpiece. Reluctantly, she pulled out the other one and looked up. Scarlett was talking to *her*. The stand-off must be over.

"Costumes are so important, don't you think?" said the other girl. "Mummy's going to organize my outfit for the British Junior Championships. A fashionista friend of hers has promised to design something totally gorgeous. I just need to decide on fabrics."

"You haven't even passed the trials yet," muttered Frankie, wishing she would shut up. She snuggled under the duvet and closed her eyes and immersed herself in a favourite daydream. Mmm… It was the one where she was performing a layback spin to the accompaniment of riotous applause.

"So?"

Frankie opened her eyes again. Couldn't the girl take a hint? Apparently not.

"Yes?" she asked wearily.

"Which one should I go for?" asked Scarlett, waving two scraps of pastel fabric in the air. "The pink or the lilac? Hmm?" She waited barely a second for a reply before launching her attack. "Oh, I'm sorry!" she said, with barely contained glee. "There I am banging on about custom-made designer outfits, when you'll be scrabbling around in the hand-me-down bin. What a shame."

What was an even bigger shame, as far as Frankie was concerned, was that she couldn't lay her hands on a roll of gaffer tape right now. Gagging Scarlett was quite clearly the only way of shutting her up. Wistfully, she thought back to the silent treatment of the past couple of weeks. It was far preferable to this stream of mean comments.

Frankie smiled sweetly. "Actually," she lied, "I haven't given my outfit a second thought. I've been concentrating on the routine. If I'm lucky enough to get through the trials, I'm sure that's what the judges at the British Junior Championships will *really* be interested in, rather than what I'm wearing."

There was a muffled snigger from Alesha's bunk.

Scarlett sniffed angrily. "I don't know what you're laughing at, Miss Death-Drop," she snapped. "You won't be upright on the ice long enough for anyone to see what you've got on."

There was no reply. But Frankie was cheered immeasurably by the fact that Alesha had laughed. It was the cheeriest sound she'd uttered since the trials had been announced. Frankie grinned. She thought for a moment and then decided that she couldn't let Scarlett have the last word, not when she'd been so rotten to Alesha. "I'd go for the pink option," she said innocently.

"Mmm," murmured Scarlett, smoothing the scrap of satin. "Do you think so? Pink does suit me…"

"Definitely," said Frankie. "And get the fashionista to add extra sequins. If it's super-sparkly, the judges might be so dazzled that they won't notice your skating." She turned over and burrowed her head deep into the duvet to hide her giggles. "Night!"

There was an angry snort before Scarlett flipped the lights off.

Frankie stretched out in the darkness, lacing her fingers behind her head. She did care, of course. She would rather be wearing something brand-spanking new, made especially for her. But that wasn't going to happen. Her parents couldn't afford to kit her out with something from London Fashion Week, not like Scarlett's mum. Which left her with Madame's fabled hand-me-down bin.

Costumes were meant to complement the music. Frankie had chosen Ravel's "Bolero" in homage to Torvill and Dean. What were the chances of her finding something second-hand to suit such a sombre, dramatic piece? It was no good skating to serious classical music wearing a clown's outfit…

The next morning, as she did every morning, Frankie crept out of the room before anyone else was up. They were fast approaching November and the depths of winter now. At this time of the morning, it was pitch-black and cold enough to make her eyes water on the way to the ice rink. Secretly, she was hoping for snow, but there was no sign yet.

After a punishing – but thrilling – ninety minutes of rocker turns, Frankie took a deep, chilly breath and asked the question that had been nagging at her since long before Scarlett had announced her silk-or-satin dilemma.

"Madame?" she asked.

"Yes?" The coach was brisk and businesslike this

morning, showing no evidence of her dreamy self from last week's lesson. "What is it? I have a meeting with Milly to discuss her British Junior Championships routine in" – she looked at her watch – "four minutes. Hurry up, girl."

"It's about the British Junior Championships, actually," said Frankie. "I, er, wondered…you see, the thing is, I—"

"Yes?"

"If I get through the trials…"

"Yes?"

"I…er…" Frankie took a deep breath. "I don't have anything to wear."

Madame Kristiana von Berne smiled, less of an ogre now. "My dear," she said, "I am well aware of that. But as a priority, it ranks somewhere below well-fitting boots and an appropriate choice of music. And a dazzling routine, we mustn't forget that." She gave a tinkling laugh. "Rest assured, those of you who get through the trials will be suitably attired for the championships. In fact, if you are successful, you will be invited for an appointment with our prestigious wardrobe department – his name is Stefan – in a couple of weeks. Until then, I suggest that you concentrate on making sure that your exits are as smooth as satin. They are infinitely more important than what you will be wearing."

Frankie didn't need a mirror to know that she was blushing. Quickly, she nodded, then exited the rink as smoothly as she knew how.

It was a Saturday, Frankie's favourite day of the week. Today, there would be the usual early morning tuition and afternoon ice-practice, but no lessons. Which left four precious hours when she wasn't expected to be anywhere or do anything.

After practising her bracket turns – yet again – with Madame, Frankie decided that she deserved a break. And she knew exactly what she was going to do with it. She smiled to herself as she helped herself to a bowl of cereal and a croissant and an orange juice and a yogurt and a bacon sandwich – it was incredible how many calories skating burned up. This morning, she would hop onto the school's minibus and venture into the local town for the first time. She had a very important purchase to make.

She glanced at her watch. The minibus would be zigzagging its way down the mountain pass in ten minutes. Perfect. That gave her just enough time to gobble the rest of her breakfast and… Hang on! Frankie spotted Alesha queuing up at the breakfast buffet. She bit hungrily into her croissant and watched as the glum-faced girl suspiciously prodded an unripe pear. She *had* to do something. And she had to do it today. Okay, so every single one of her attempts to cheer Alesha up had been rebuffed so far. But that was no excuse for giving up.

"Yoohoo!" she called impetuously.

Alesha turned.

"I've saved you a space!" Frankie grinned and pointed to the empty seat beside her.

And, perhaps because the packed canteen wasn't the best place for a hissy fit or maybe because she was just tired of ignoring everyone, Alesha grabbed a cereal bar and wove between the tables until she reached Frankie.

"You okay?" she muttered.

Frankie nodded vehemently. This was going well. Two words was a vast improvement on none. "I'm popping into Friedelsberg after breakfast," she said. "Fancy it?" To her immense surprise, Alesha nodded.

"It's less than two weeks to the trials," Alesha said, her tone flat. "They'll probably be my last. If I fall flat on my face again, I'm out. I'd better get some souvenirs for Mum and Dad while I have the chance."

Ignoring the bulk of her gloomy reply, Frankie pounced on one word. "Souvenirs!" she said brightly. "Just what I was thinking. I need to find a cuckoo clock for my mum, you see. If I go back to London without one, I'll be strung up. Come on, you can eat that on the way!" Grabbing Alesha's arm, she bundled her out of the canteen, through the warren of corridors and onto the minibus.

In no time at all, they were descending towards Friedelsberg. It was picture-postcard pretty, with narrow, twisty streets of wooden chalets. In summer, the quaint town was rammed with tourists. But, by late autumn, the crowds were long gone. Today, the locals were milling about the marketplace, choosing from the array of glossy vegetables for sale.

"Wonderful, isn't it?" said Frankie, standing on the pavement as the minibus drove away from them.

Alesha gave a brief, unhappy nod.

Crikey, this was difficult. Frankie rustled up her cheeriest grin in an attempt to break the deadlock. Then, when this elicited no response, she tried again.

"Look—"

"I'm sorry—"

Frankie and Alesha spoke at exactly the same time, words bashing into each other like rugby players. They both giggled.

"Don't be daft," said Frankie. "There's nothing to apologize for." She flung an arm around her friend's shoulder. "Are you going to help me find the tackiest cuckoo clock in the whole of Switzerland or what?"

"I am," replied Alesha.

The four hours that had stretched endlessly away from Frankie suddenly became far too short. Her silence broken at last, Alesha gabbled non-stop. And together, they trawled the shops for souvenirs, eventually finding a collection of snow globes for Alesha to take home and a small wooden cuckoo clock for Frankie's mum. The cuckoo popped out to sing every fifteen minutes – it was sure to send the entire family bonkers within hours.

"Excellent!" said Frankie delightedly.

It was just the tonic Alesha needed. Over a hefty slice of gooey Sachertorte, she admitted to Frankie that she was thoroughly bored of being miserable now. And even though she might not get through the trials, she was going to give it her best shot – and do her level best not to fall over. But if she did, she wasn't going to get stressed out about it.

"Yay!" said Frankie, not caring that her teeth were smeared with chocolate cake crumbs. Her friend was back!

Chapter *Seventeen*

Frankie spent every spare minute practising her routine in the last two weeks before the trials. Devised by Madame, who vetoed all of the wildly adventurous moves that her eager pupil wanted to include, it was a sequence of graceful moves punctuated by the obligatory spins and jumps that the judges would be watching out for.

"Why can't I do a triple toe-loop?" pleaded Frankie, one chilly November morning, when Madame had sniffed at her request to include it in the routine. A triple toe-loop was a challenging jump, but an impressive one. It would show that she could skate with the best of them. And she knew she could do it – she just needed Madame to show her how.

"Because you're not ready," was the no-nonsense reply. "The double toe-loop is perfect for you right now. Any more than that would be foolish."

Frankie was stunned. How was she expected to compete with the others when her routine was going to be made up of beginner jumps and basic turns? Faced with Madame's stern glare, she bit back her disappointment and took to the ice. She would listen to the coaching director, for now. But she wasn't planning on forgetting about the triple toe-loop.

Far, far too soon, it was time for the trials. They were held on a Tuesday afternoon in November. The judges were Madame von Berne, Rob Pearson and Ally Williams. And the audience was everyone not taking part.

Nervously, Frankie waited with the others in the locker room as the sound of Rimsky-Korsakov's "Flight of the Bumblebee" buzzed through the closed doors.

"What possessed Milly to pick such a frantic piece of music?" breathed Alesha, who looked as terrified as if she were about to perform in front of a firing squad.

Frankie shook her head. "Dunno," she said. "But if anyone can pull it off, Milly can. She's a fantastic skater." It was true. Quiet, unassuming Milly was quietly brilliant. Her moves were fluid, yet controlled. And she wasn't afraid to take risks.

"I think she's just showing off," huffed Scarlett, flinging back her mane of blonde hair as she retied the satin bows in her figure skates.

Woody guffawed with laughter. "Of course she's showing off!" he said. "That's what we're *all* meant to be doing, you doughnut."

Everyone but Scarlett – whose cheeks were now as colourful as her name – chuckled briefly, before they all resumed their grim expressions. Within a few minutes, the music ended and, shortly after, Milly reappeared.

"I'm glad that's over," she said, grinning with relief.

"Well…?" asked Paul.

"I'm through," said Milly, blushing. "I didn't land properly on the triple toe-loop jump, but my Lutz was okay."

There was a chorus of "Well done"s and "Congratulations", which made Milly blush all the more. Quickly changing out of her boots, she made her excuses and left.

"Doesn't like a fuss, our Milly," said Dylan. "She'll be hopeless when she gets a medal, poor girl."

Scarlett tutted.

Then the door swung open again and Woody was called through to face the music.

To Frankie, it suddenly seemed that everything was now going far, far too quickly. A feeling of panic welled up inside her. No, no, no…not yet! She might have practised her routine until she could do it in her sleep, but she wasn't quite ready. If only she had more time. Just a couple more days to polish her Salchow, that was all she needed—

Woody clattered back through the swing doors, his cheeks rosy with exhaustion. "I'm through, just." He heaved an enormous sigh of relief.

Paul wasn't so lucky. "I fluffed it…" he groaned, limping back into the locker room minutes later, helped by Rob the coach. "Caught an edge and cartwheeled into the barrier. Cool move, but it wasn't in the programme. And then my ankle packed in on landing. Ouch!" He grinned ruefully as he tugged at his laces. "Do excuse me, I have an appointment with the nurse…"

Bethany fared no better. As the sounds of the classic flute tune "Annie's Song" faded away, she burst through the doors in floods of tears. It was impossible to work out exactly what had happened, but between sniffs and hiccups, it appeared that the disaster involved "over-rotation" and "double Salchow".

Frankie gulped. There was a double Salchow in her own routine. Not the triple that she dreamed of, but a daring move all the same. Frankie *loved* it. She planned to follow it with a double toe-loop, before launching into the final spin of her routine – a layback spin – but if the double Salchow went wrong, it would throw everything else out. It was *vital* that she didn't slip up.

One by one, the skaters were swallowed by the swing doors, which spat them out again a few minutes later.

Flic returned, beaming from ear to ear.

"No prizes for guessing that you passed!" said Dylan, slapping her on the back.

Scarlett gave a tight smile. "Yeah, well done," she muttered. Then her name was called and she swiftly made her way towards the rink.

Frankie tried to swallow, but her throat was too dry. Not long now… Their names had been drawn out of a hat and she was going last of all. It was better than being first, but not much. By the time she had her turn, the ice would be like a ploughed field. It would be much easier to catch an edge or be thrown off balance.

The swing door was punched open as Scarlett

made her entrance, striding through the changing room as gracefully as her skates would allow. "I skated brilliantly," she boasted. "I'm going to London!"

"Well done," said Dylan, with a low chuckle and a shake of his head. "Who's showing off now?" he asked Frankie, under his breath. Then, "Uh-oh, it's my turn."

Frankie watched him go, feeling a rush of nerves. She so hoped he'd get through, because he'd worked *incredibly* hard.

"Hurray!" squeaked Flic, rushing forward to hug Scarlett. "Wouldn't it be *wonderful* if we got silver and gold medals?!"

"Wonderful," agreed Scarlett, pulling away slightly. "But you don't mind having silver, do you? Gold goes so much better with my hair!" She gave a hearty laugh. "I'm joking, of course."

Flic laughed uncertainly.

Then Bethany, who sat forgotten and forlorn in a corner of the locker room, gave a small whimper and they both rushed over to console her.

Frankie gulped. She patted Alesha gently on the

shoulder. The girl seemed entirely oblivious to the goings-on in the locker room and beyond. Shivering with fear, she looked up from the wooden bench on which she was perched. "Is it me?" she muttered.

"You're next," said Frankie. She grasped Alesha's hand and smiled encouragingly. "You'll be *fine*. Just go out there and do your best."

Dylan returned, greeting them all with a modest nod and a smile that showed he'd survived the trials too. He grinned at Alesha as she trudged past him. "Go, girl!" he said enthusiastically. "You can do it."

And she did. Afterwards, looking dazed and confused, yet very happy, Alesha sank down onto a bench and just beamed.

So now, finally, it was Frankie's turn. There was barely time for her to give Alesha a quick hug, before she had to go. Robot-like, she marched towards the swing doors and – *wham-bam!* – heard them shut behind her. Momentarily dazzled by the lights, she took a deep breath and waited for her eyes to adjust.

In the front row, with the best view in the house,

were the three coaches – Madame von Berne, Ally Williams and Rob Pearson. These were the people that Frankie had to impress.

Tentatively, she stepped onto the ice and skated steadily towards the centre of the rink, before coming to a neat stop and striking her opening pose.

"Ready?" asked Madame.

Frankie nodded. This was it. Never had she felt so scared *or* so exhilarated.

Without another word, the coaching director signalled for the music to start.

The familiar bars of Ravel's "Bolero" surged around the arena and Frankie pushed off on one foot, beginning her routine with a smoothly executed pull-up spin. So far so good. She began to relax, the moves so ingrained into her subconscious that she hardly had to think about what came next. She just knew.

And then pure enjoyment took over. She sprang into the air with a graceful stag jump, left knee tucked beneath her and right leg extended, her arms held wide. She landed safely, completed a perfect three-turn to reverse her direction, before back crossovers whisked her round the rink, not too close, yet not too far from the perimeter. Before she knew it, Frankie was preparing for her final combination of jumps.

First came the double Salchow.

Skating backwards on her left foot, she bent her knee and sprang upwards, her right arm and leg swinging round and round. As her toe pick left the ice, she felt her centre of gravity change in mid-air from left to right before she made contact with the ice again, this time with her right toe pick, and then with a frosty whoosh she was gliding backwards...

...and straight into the double toe-loop. As her toe pick stuck into the ice, her left knee bent and then straightened powerfully, propelling her upwards once more. Briefly, time slowed and she seemed to hang in the air like a puppet on wires, slowly rotating twice until, with a gentle *dink* she landed again, on the right outside edge.

Frankie felt like whooping for joy and for a moment her concentration wavered. She felt her right skate wobble as it hit a particularly deep rut. *Was she going to fall?* With determined strokes, she steadied herself. Phew... She *mustn't* lose it now, not so close to the end. Her composure regained, she entered the final spin of the routine.

Gently turning on her left skate, she pushed her hips forward and began to lean her upper body backwards until her neck and head followed suit, finally bringing her arms upwards until she was spinning, spinning, spinning...a blur of arms and legs.

And then it was over.

Frankie came to a neat halt as the music faded away. She curtsied politely to the judges, who consulted their notes and spoke quietly to each other, while she wondered vaguely if this was what it was like to be tortured. Luckily, she didn't have long to wait.

Madame nodded briskly. "Good," she said, with the merest hint of a smile. "You'd better get yourself an outfit sorted," she continued. "You're going to the British Junior Championships!"

CHAPTER *Eighteen*

To: mumndadnjoshnjessnmeg
From: Frankieonthemove
Subject: YAYYYY!

Lutz-loop-tastic! I'm through! Nearly fluffed it when I landed after the double toe-loop, but managed to stay upright, thank Torvill. Hurray! So just another three weeks and I'll be coming to London to compete in the British Junior Championships. Don't suppose there's a spare bed at the Wills B&B, is there?

See you soooooon!

Love,

Frankie X

It was like the best birthday present *and* the best Christmas present rolled into one. Frankie couldn't remember when she'd been this thrilled – not even when she'd won the place at the Ice Palace. Then, she'd felt as if she were perched at the top of a massive rollercoaster. Excited? *Yes*. Apprehensive? *Definitely*. But now that she'd experienced the dizzying highs – and, yes, the plummeting lows – of figure skating, Frankie knew just how totally wonderful it was to do what you loved most in the whole world every single day of every week. She felt as if she were still on that rollercoaster, as it looped and spun towards the championships in London. There was no way she wanted to get off.

"Penny for them?"

"Huh?" Jolted from an enjoyable reverie just before she touched down after a triple Lutz, she looked up guiltily. "Just daydreaming," she said. "Nothing special."

"Yeah, right," said Alesha, with a chuckle. She was totally back on form after her success at the trials and Frankie, for one, was delighted. Now, she looked pointedly at her watch. "Isn't there somewhere you should be?" Alesha asked.

Frankie scrunched up her nose as she thought. Training? Lessons? Extra lessons? Extra training? She really seemed to do nothing else at the moment.

"Stefan?" prompted Alesha.

"Argh!" cried Frankie, remembering her appointment with the wardrobe department. "I'm late!"

"No, you're not," said Alesha. "You're just on time. If you go *now*!"

Frankie went.

"Oooooh," she breathed, smoothing her fingers over the silky fabric. "It's lovely…"

"Black is so miserable," said Stefan, the wardrobe

manager. "Are you sure you don't want to go with the lime green?" He looked more than a little disappointed. "It would go so well with your complexion…"

"Maybe next time," said Frankie. "If there *is* one."

"Oh, there *will* be a next time," said Stefan, nodding vehemently. "From what I hear, you'd give Katarina Witt a run for her money." He smiled wistfully, as if remembering the glamorous German figure skater. "Her version of 'Carmen' was phenomenal and her outfit was divine… Can't I persuade you to wear red instead? With a few frills?"

Frankie had watched the clip of Katarina on YouTube only last week. She was one of her idols and to be likened to her was incredibly flattering. But Frankie remembered the photo of Madame von Berne in the entrance hall and knew that she wanted to wear black, like her. "If there is a next time, I'll wear whatever you like," she promised.

He brightened immediately. "Excellent!" he said, picking up the dark fabric and eyeing it critically. "In the meantime, I'll see what I can do with this…

Perhaps a sprinkling of sequins and some ruffles might help…" he added doubtfully.

Frankie sneaked out and rejoined the others in the common room. There, Scarlett was holding court, telling Flic, Bethany and anyone else who would listen about the designer dress that her mother had had made for her. "It's a Gambetti Poloni original," she boasted. "No one in the world will have a dress like this, you know. And Mummy took all my measurements in the summer holidays, so it'll fit like a glove."

"Never mind a glove. Put a *sock* in it!" called Paul, his bandaged ankle propped up on a sofa. "Some of us aren't even going to London. The last thing we want to hear is you banging on about it!"

Frankie smiled. Paul must be feeling better if he was answering back. He'd been rather gloomy since he wiped out at the trials. And who could blame him? He hadn't just missed out on the opportunity to compete in the British Junior Championships – he'd busted his ankle too. But at least Madame hadn't expelled him. He would be given a chance to compete in the next major event and it was only then, if he failed to shine, that he'd be saying goodbye to Team GB.

Poor Bethany wasn't so lucky. She'd been called to see Madame von Berne the day after the trials and had reappeared an hour later with red-rimmed eyes and a streaky face. After prolonged public wailing and at least a bucket of tears, Bethany revealed that she was being sent home.

"I've been given the o-o-option to stay until the end of t-t-term or leave n-n-now," she stammered, her bottom lip wobbling.

"What are you going to do?" asked Milly gently.

"I'm going now-wow-wow…" wailed Bethany. "Madame says that it's not just my skating. It's that I'm not t-t-tough enough for the world of figure skating. But she's *wrong*." She hiccuped loudly. "I *am* tough. Nothing *ever* upsets me!" Bethany flung her arms around Milly – Scarlett had legged it at the first sign of tears – and began to sob in earnest.

"She'd come in handy in a hosepipe ban," said Woody, but quietly and rather sadly.

No one wanted to gloat over a fellow skater's misfortune. They all knew that life at the Ice Palace was precarious at best. Madame had told them over and over that although she wanted to nurture them as figure skaters and encourage them to be the best they could be, her focus was Team GB. It had to be. And it wasn't just skating ability that she needed. Figure skaters had to put in the endless hours of hard work necessary to be champions. They also had to be tough enough to withstand the knocks that came with international competition. Those who crumbled at the first sign of difficulty would never make it onto the Olympic podium.

Skating wasn't just sequins and twirls. It was hard work too.

Bethany left later that evening, still gulping and hiccuping as she clambered into the taxi. They all waved as the car rumbled away from the training school.

That night, Frankie lay awake for hours. She was wildly excited about going to the British Junior Championships, but she thought about poor Bethany too, flying home tonight with her dreams of Olympic success in tatters.

It could so easily happen to any of them.

But if there was one thing Frankie knew, it was that she was going to try *really* hard to make sure that it didn't happen to her.

Chapter *Nineteen*

Time whizzed by in a blur of practice, routines, lessons, costume fittings, practice, and more practice, until there were less than ten days to go until the junior figure skaters left for London.

Frankie had polished her routine until it shone. But even though it contained all the obligatory jumps and spins, she couldn't help feeling that something was missing. Madame might be happy with it, but Frankie wasn't. Why couldn't she swap the double toe-loop for a triple? She *knew* she could do it.

"If it ain't broke, don't fix it," advised Dylan, when she explained to him what she thought her routine was lacking. "I've watched you skate," he went on, "and it looked pretty perfect to me. I spotted all the required elements. What more do you want?"

"I don't just want to satisfy the requirements…" insisted Frankie. "I want to be better than that. I want to be *daring*."

"Sometimes, you don't need to be daring," said Dylan patiently. "The judges are assessing skating skills, transitions, performance, choreography and interpretation. It's only a short programme. Save your dazzling stuff for another competition."

Frankie sighed. If Dylan wasn't going to listen, the chances were nobody would. They all wanted her to skate a nice little programme that ticked all the boxes. She was new, they said. There was plenty of time for her to experiment with the adventurous stuff when she was more experienced. This time, it was more important for her to play it safe, rather than risk everything with tricky moves that might go horribly wrong.

But Frankie wanted to shine. *Really* shine. She didn't want to disobey Madame, but she didn't want to fade into the background either. How did she stand a chance against pros like Scarlett and Milly if her routine was basic and boring? So secretly, she began to practise the triple toe-loop. Just in case. If Madame changed her mind, she'd be ready. And if Frankie felt brave – or foolish – enough on the day, then the triple toe-loop would be polished and ready to shine.

There were no prizes for guessing that the triple toe-loop was very like a double toe-loop jump, but it had more spin – with three full revolutions – and was much more difficult. Which made it, as far as Frankie was concerned, so much more impressive.

It was surprisingly hard perfecting the jump without Madame's constant, nit-picking comments. Just a little higher here… No, no, no… More rotation! Frankie could almost imagine them, but it wasn't quite the same. Still, she tried and tried again until she thought she might have cracked it.

After lessons the next afternoon, just five days before they were due to leave, she persuaded Alesha to come to the rink to check out her jump.

"What do you think?" she asked afterwards.

"Brilliant…" said Alesha. "It's loads better than mine."

Frankie shook her head quickly. She wasn't asking for *ooh*s and *aah*s – that wouldn't improve her skating. "Don't be daft," she muttered. Then, "Seriously, is there any way I could improve it?"

Alesha rubbed her chin. "Okay, if you want me to be really critical, you might want to try bending your knee a little more when you touch down, just to make doubly sure that it's a good, solid landing. You don't want to be slithering across the ice afterwards." She patted Frankie on the shoulder. "And you might want to add a smile. Look like you're enjoying yourself. I'm *sure* the judges deduct points from skaters who look as if they're sucking lemons. Otherwise, as I said, it's brilliant."

"Thanks so much," said Frankie gratefully. "I can't ask Madame, you see," she explained. "She wants me to stick to the boring old double toe-loop. And that isn't going to impress anyone." She pivoted on one toe.

Immediately, Alesha looked nervous. "What?" she said. "You don't mean that you're including it in your routine…? But Madame said you shouldn't." She bit her lip. "Look, if Madame doesn't think you should do something, then you can't. You just *can't*. She would be totally livid. She might send you *home*."

"Hey, don't worry," backtracked Frankie. "I didn't say I was going to do it. I just thought I might, that's all."

Alesha still looked worried. "Just stick to the programme," she said.

"Come on," said Frankie, gliding towards the barrier and clumping on to dry land. "Let's go and see if Stefan's finished our outfits."

Relieved at the change of subject, Alesha nodded. "Good plan. I hope he hasn't made mine too girly. He kept harping on about frills and bows. That's just *so* not me."

Frankie chuckled to herself. New, confident Alesha might be toeing the line this week, but glimmers of the old subversive Alesha kept appearing, enough to reassure her that her friend hadn't changed that much. But she resolved to keep quiet about her triple toe-loop from now on. It was something she had to decide for herself. There was no point worrying anyone else.

It was when they were a good two hundred metres from Stefan's office that they heard the bloodcurdling scream.

"What was *that*?" demanded Frankie, before she and Alesha legged it towards the sound. By the time they reached the wardrobe department, the scream had downgraded into ragged sobs and they were stunned to find that these were coming from Scarlett, who was clinging on to a scared-looking Stefan for grim death. He shrugged helplessly at them.

"What's wrong?" asked Frankie softly.

"It's my outfit…" gasped Scarlett. "The one I was going to wear when I win the British Junior Championships!"

Alesha rolled her eyes. "Hmm?" she prompted.

"My Gambetti Poloni original is…is…"

"Yes?" asked Frankie.

"A child's tutu!" roared Scarlett. The outraged girl started pumping out new rivulets of tears. "I *hate* it! I wanted to be the Queen of the Ice, not a Sugar Plum Fairy!"

Frankie bit her lip in an effort not to laugh as Scarlett shook the pink ball of lace and tulle like a giant pompom. "Stefan, you *must* make me something else!" she demanded.

Stefan nodded seriously, but his eyes danced. "There isn't much time..." he murmured.

"Anything!" shrieked Scarlett.

He relented. "I'll see what I can do."

"Gambetti Poloni!" spat Scarlett. "I'll stick to Christian Dior from now on!"

And then there were only two days to go before the British Junior Championships. It was the end of November now and winter had blanketed the green mountainsides with a layer of snow. It wasn't much, just a few centimetres so far. But it was enough to build a very small snowman. And it was a hint of what was to come.

Dylan told Frankie cheerfully that they would probably be snowed in.

"How will we get to London, then?" she asked.

"Ah," replied Dylan. "Hadn't thought of that."

Frankie had never spent a winter in the Alps and she hoped desperately that she would do well enough in London to be allowed back to enjoy it.

She was still in two minds about the toe-loop jump. The double or the triple? The triple or the double…? Was it worth risking a place on the podium by sticking with the bog-standard, so-easy-that-she-could-do-it-in-her-sleep double toe-loop? Was it worth risking her place at the Ice Palace by disobeying Madame and going for the triple…?

Frankie just didn't know.

Chapter *Twenty*

Friday arrived at last.

"Morning!" cried Woody, bashing on the girls' door as he thundered down the corridor and past their room. "We're leaving on a jet plane! Woohoo!"

There was no chance of him disturbing Frankie. She'd been awake for hours and wasn't entirely sure she'd slept at all. She'd gone over and over the routine in her head so many times that she couldn't think straight. At least she didn't have to take responsibility for her outfit. Madame had decided to look after these for safe keeping. Frankie would be given her dress back before the event.

At breakfast, Madame treated them all to a speech peppered with uplifting phrases. *Do your best… Reach for the sky… Show them what you can do!*

"No pressure there, then," said Frankie.

"Nah," said Dylan. "As long as you win, you'll be fine."

Frankie managed a watery smile.

"Hey, at least you'll be seeing your folks," he added cheerily.

At this, Frankie brightened considerably. It had been eight long weeks and she'd missed her family, especially her mum and dad. She'd even missed her brother, whose favourite sport was winding her up. Since she'd last seen them, the twins had apparently learned to walk and were now "into everything", whatever that meant. Apparently, they were also really good at spraying the kitchen walls with soggy Weetabix.

"They're going to be plasterers when they grow

up, mark my words," her dad had said proudly on the phone. "Looking forward to seeing you, sweetie," he'd added.

Frankie couldn't wait. But she couldn't help thinking that the Frankie they welcomed home wouldn't be the same Frankie they'd waved off. In eight weeks, she'd changed from a hobby skater to a serious competitor. Where once she'd dreamed of being a proper figure skater, now she couldn't help dreaming of Olympic gold. Skating was her top priority, as it had always been. She loved it so, *so* much. But gradually, as she'd learned jumps that thrilled her, and spins that made her buzz with excitement, she'd realized that she wanted to be the best too.

Saying goodbye to the others was unexpectedly emotional. Paul, who was now hobbling around on a set of crutches, gave them firm handshakes and wished them luck in a gruff voice.

"You might stand a chance of winning if I'm not there," he told Dylan and Woody. "Break a leg, won't you?"

"Yeah, right…" muttered Woody.

"Packed your tutu?" Paul asked Scarlett, eyes dancing with mirth.

Ignoring him totally, she marched off in the direction of the minibus with her designer luggage. Rumour had it that Stefan had rustled her up a brown and green number in the last couple of days, claiming that he'd run out of all the other colours.

Scarlett was *not* happy about it.

Frankie flashed Paul a smile. "Get well soon, right?" she said. "Hopefully, I'll see you after the weekend."

"Oh, you'll see me all right," said the invalid, with more confidence than Frankie felt. "There's no way you'll be allowed to escape the Ice Palace, not now that Madame von Berne has got her claws into you. You're in it for the long haul, matey!" His smile stiffened. "Hi, Madame!" he said, as the coaching director appeared, clad in a long, tweed coat and furry Russian hat. "Have a good trip…"

Frankie was so touched by his words that she nearly burst into tears, but she gulped them back, waved goodbye to Paul and all the older students who'd gathered to wish them luck, and climbed up the steps after Scarlett.

Minutes later, the seven students and Madame were trundling down the narrow mountain road, winter tyres making a soft *brrrrr* noise on the fresh snow. With the exception of the coaching director and Scarlett – who was idly flicking through *Vogue* magazine as if nothing were more important to her than discovering the ideal skirt length this season – everyone was trying their best not to look nervous. Flic looked over Scarlett's shoulder, trying to read her magazine. Dylan and Woody sprawled across the back seat, talking loudly about 4x4s, while Alesha, Milly and Frankie alternately chewed their fingernails and discussed the finer points of the Bauer – one of the most graceful moves on ice.

In no time at all, they were checking in at Zurich Airport…boarding the plane…and soaring above soft, billowing fields of cloud. Where, on the outbound journey, Frankie had felt as if her old life was becoming less real, now the same was happening to her new life in Switzerland. She was going back to reality, and leaving the Ice Palace far, far behind.

* * *

"Yay!" hollered Josh across the arrivals concourse. "She's here!"

"Who on earth is that idiot?" muttered Scarlett. "Does anyone know him?"

"I do!" sang Frankie, not caring a jot what Scarlett thought. "He's my brother."

"Figures," said Scarlett.

Immediately, Frankie was squished inside a monster hug that contained every member of her family and more arms than a mythical creature, and the twins squealed so loudly that she began to wonder if they'd be arrested for disturbing the peace.

"See you at Alexandra Palace tomorrow for training," said Madame as she strode past, heels tapping on the concourse. "Don't be late."

"Yes!" shouted Frankie, struggling to make herself heard above the furore. "Bye!" This was to the other students, who were being similarly suffocated by their families.

This wasn't usual practice, Madame had told

them. The ideal scenario was that all the skaters stayed at the same hotel, away from all outside influences. There, they could really focus on the upcoming competition. The problem was, their hotel had been double-booked. Those who lived outside London were being accommodated in B&Bs near Alexandra Palace, but they'd decided that locals like Frankie may as well go home.

"No rest for the wicked…" said Dad, lugging her suitcase onto a trolley. He shook his head in a confused way as the trolley began to make curious *u-ooo-u-ooo* noises. "Don't you even get a day off?"

Frankie shook her head. "Madame von Berne wants us to get to know the ice rink at Alexandra Palace," she said. "She says it's important that we feel relaxed when we perform on Sunday. Talking of which…" She reached into her pocket and pulled out a white envelope, which she handed to her mum.

Not one for suspense, Mrs. Wills ripped it open and gazed at the silver-and-white tickets that lay inside. "British Junior Championships…" she said dazedly. "Front-row seats!"

"Of course," said Frankie, knowing that she would be more nervous than ever to have her entire family rinkside. But she also knew that she wouldn't want them to be anywhere else. "So, will you come?"

The reply was deafening.

Chapter *Twenty-one*

THUD! Thud-thud-thud. Thud-*thud*.

"Josh!" Mum hollered at the ceiling. "Are you auditioning for *Riverdance* up there?"

"Waaaaaaaaah!" wailed the twins.

"If only there was a mute button I could press…" groaned Dad. Frankie calmly went on eating her cereal. It was *so* good to be home – although she couldn't help wishing that she had a pair of earplugs. She'd forgotten how totally LOUD her family could be. She'd only been in Switzerland for a couple of months, but it already seemed as if home had changed immeasurably. The twins yabbered non-stop, spending every spare moment shredding tissue paper and popping any loose objects down the toilet. Josh was taller and he was smellier, too, in an aftershave-meets-tree-shaped-air-freshener type of way. It was enough to make your eyes water.

"So, how are you feeling this fine, bright Sunday morning?" asked Mum. "Are you ready to wow us with your triple flip-flop today?"

"I think so…" Frankie said, deciding to ignore her mum's shocking grasp of skating terms. She wasn't quite sure if she was ready or not. On the one hand, she just wanted to get on with it. On the other, she couldn't help wondering if she should have practised just that little bit more. The British Junior Championships were important for so many reasons. It was her first real competition. She'd be performing in front of her first crowd, wearing her first proper outfit… And the stomach-clenching dilemma of the double toe-loop versus the triple toe-loop still hadn't been resolved. What should she *do*?

Saturday's practice at Alexandra Palace hadn't helped Frankie to make a decision either way. She'd stumbled through her routine three times – each performance worse than the last. By the end of the session, she couldn't even do a single toe-loop, never mind a double or a triple. Madame had reassured her that it was simply a case of nerves, but Frankie wasn't so sure. Meanwhile, Scarlett did one flawless performance after another.

Now, Frankie shivered as she remembered the utter desolation she'd felt as Scarlett sailed past, smiling gleefully at Frankie, who was spreadeagled on the ice after yet another failed jump. She wanted to beat Scarlett *so* badly. But how could she do it when her routine was so dull?

The competition wasn't due to start until two that afternoon, although Madame von Berne insisted that all of her Olympic hopefuls should be there a good two hours early to allow for delays with public transport – Mr. Wills snorted at this – and to give them plenty of time to warm up. It was decided that Frankie should go on ahead and that her family would follow. There'd be no chance for her to see them at Ally Pally before the performance, so they all wished her luck now. Mum was overcome by emotion again, sobbing all over her, while Dad squeezed all the air out of her with a hug worthy of a grizzly bear. It was almost a relief to go, although Frankie had to gulp repeatedly to avoid sobbing. She was about to compete in her very first figure-skating competition and her family would be there. She so wanted them to be proud of her.

"Bye!" she said quickly, before hurrying to the bus stop.

Contrary to Madame's expectations of London's public transport system, the journey was seamless. Frankie was the first to arrive. She clambered off the bus and gazed up at wonderful old Alexandra Palace, sat atop a gentle hill with breathtaking views of London. The palace itself dated back to Victorian times. It was built of brick, was wide, sprawling and very ornate.

Frankie stared and stared. Never had Ally Pally looked quite so wonderful as it did today, the late-autumn sun dyeing the antique brickwork a glorious pinky-orange.

"Wow," she breathed, before reluctantly tearing her eyes from the sprawling building and trudging up the hill towards the grand entrance.

Unsurprisingly, Madame was there before her.

"Ah, Frankie," she said, very businesslike. "Stefan had some final alterations to make to your outfit. You'll be pleased to know that I have it here." Slowly, the coach reached into her leather holdall and pulled out a pink-tissue parcel. She gave it to Frankie.

Frankie stared at the precious package in her hands.

"Open it, then," said Madame, her voice softer now.

With trembling fingers, Frankie pulled back the tissue to reveal ebony silk dotted with sequins. It gleamed like a starry sky, the silky fabric cool and slippery in her hands. It was the stuff of dreams. "Thank you," she breathed, realizing that now was the time to broach the topic of the jumps. She opened her mouth and—

"Kristiana!" interrupted a piercing voice. A large woman bundled up in a silvery fake-fur coat clattered towards them on noisy heels. "It *is* you, isn't it? I didn't know you would be here! It's been such a long time."

"It is me and I am here, as you can see," said Madame coolly. "I'm afraid that I was just in the middle of—"

"But we must catch up!" shrieked the woman. "I haven't seen you since, er…it was *those* World Championships, wasn't it? Copenhagen? Where I got the gold and you—"

"I know exactly which championships you are talking about." Twin spots of anger highlighted Madame von Berne's powdered cheeks. She turned to Frankie. "Go and start your stretches, please," she said. "Now!"

Frankie scurried away from the foyer towards the changing rooms, straining her ears to hear what the big, brassy woman was saying. She must have been one of the other competitors in that fateful competition where Madame had crashed out of figure skating. Frankie hadn't missed the underlying boastfulness in the woman's voice either. She was doing her best to wind up the Team GB coach, to lord it over her and humiliate her. They must be rivals from the past. Bitter rivals, too.

As the changing-room door clanged shut behind her, Frankie realized with annoyance that she'd missed her last opportunity to discuss the triple toe-loop with Madame. Now she'd never know if she could have changed her mind. It was too late now. The others would be arriving soon and then it would be time to step onto the ice.

"Hi!" The door crashed open again to reveal Alesha, her face a mixture of amazement and terror. "Ooooh," she whispered. "Did you see Tatiana Dubrovich?"

"The woman in the huge fluffy coat?" said Frankie.

Alesha nodded. "I got out of the way quickly – didn't want to get caught in the crossfire…" Quickly, she told all. Frankie had been right, the two women had battled for gold in Madame's last-ever championships. They were both brilliant skaters, but everyone had always said that Madame had the edge. The triple loop was to have been the highlight of her freestyle performance – if she'd achieved it, the gold would have been hers. But, she fell. And Madame Dubrovich – now a successful coach herself – had pulled off victory with a triple Salchow instead.

"No wonder Madame looked so cross," said Frankie. So that's what had happened. Madame shouldn't have gone for the triple loop. It had been too much for her. And now she was against Frankie doing the triple toe-loop. Surely, if there were any lesson to be learned from Madame's story, it was that Frankie shouldn't overdo it... Thoughtfully, she pulled her figure skates from her holdall and paused to admire their lustrous sheen, the result of an hour's hard polishing on Saturday evening. And for a brief, wonderful second, she imagined herself wearing them as she spun round and round in a beautiful triple toe-loop.

Alesha waggled a finger at her. "This means, of course, that our coach will now be in the worst possible of moods. Please, Frankie...I can tell you're still tempted to do the triple. But if you value your future as a figure skater, *don't* do it. *Please*."

A bell rang and then a woman's voice sounded

over the loudspeaker. "Competitors, this is your ninety-minute warning."

Frankie gulped, before turning to Alesha with a reassuring smile. "Come on, we'd better do some stretching," she said. "It'll be all right," she added, deliberately avoiding the tricky subject of her double dilemma. It wasn't something that Alesha should be worrying about. It was up to Frankie to decide, and no one else.

But would it be all right? As the changing-room door crashed open to admit a whole crowd of competitors, all gossiping noisily about their routines, their outfits and how many sequins they were each wearing, Frankie realized that the time left for her to make a decision was swiftly running out.

CHAPTER *Twenty-Two*

"Who nicked my glittery eyeshadow?" roared Scarlett, her outraged voice rising above the hubbub in the girls' changing room.

By now, just fifteen minutes before the competition began, there were twenty-odd girls in there. The air was filled with squeals, whoops and a fine mist of hairspray. Outfits hung from every hook, the shiny fabric like a silken rainbow. Frankie had never been anywhere so totally inspiring and completely terrifying in her life.

"It's bad enough that I have to wear this monstrosity, without my make-up vanishing too!" continued Scarlett. She stood with her hands on her hips, so angry that nearby competitors shrank away from her.

"Hmm…" said Alesha, not fazed in the slightest. "So *that's* your outfit. Hey, at least you can wear it on safari afterwards."

Scarlett smoothed manicured fingers down her deeply unfashionable dress – made of a mixture of green and brown silk, with cap sleeves, a sticky-out skirt and a high neck – and just growled.

Luckily, and before a fight broke out, Frankie spotted a shiny compact near Scarlett's bag. "Is that it?" she asked, pointing to the floor.

"Hmph," said Scarlett. Without a word of thanks, she grabbed the make-up and span round to face the mirror, where she began daubing her eyelids with green glitter.

If she hadn't been quite so nervous, Frankie would have laughed. As it was, she was far more concerned with her own appearance. Yes, she knew that it was the skating that counted with the judges, but that didn't stop her worrying about ripping seams and snagging her tights. And how much make-up should she wear? Too little make-up and the audience wouldn't see it. Too much make-up and she'd look like a clown. In the end, Frankie settled for a shimmery blue eyeshadow, heavy-duty mascara and a touch of lipgloss. She'd also managed to sweep her hair into a respectable chignon, which was held in place by a handful of clips and a frighteningly large amount of hairspray.

"That looks perfect," said Alesha, as if guessing her thoughts. "Now for your dress!"

Reverently, Frankie lifted her very first competition outfit from its hook. The black silk flowed coolly over her fingers and she couldn't help a shiver of excitement as she slipped it over her head.

It had a scooped neck and long sleeves, each ending with a pointed cuff. The bodice was fitted, while the short skirt flared gently outwards.

And it fitted like a dream.

"Wow," said Alesha. "Go get 'em, girl!"

* * *

As luck would have it, Frankie was on the ice first out of the eighteen competitors. There were just seven of them from the Ice Palace – Alesha, Milly, Flic, Scarlett, Woody, Dylan and Frankie – with the remaining entrants coming from regional ice-skating clubs. As Madame had reminded her pupils so many times, they were expected to do well. They were the best of the best, destined for Olympic glory. If they couldn't succeed at national level, what hope was there for them at the bigger events…?

Frankie took deep breaths, reminding herself that being first was no big deal. She'd spent the six-minute on-ice warm-up wisely. The rink would be smooth. She wouldn't have to hang around in the changing room for hours waiting for her turn. Although, now that the moment was upon her, she would have given anything to be last.

"Break a leg," drawled Scarlett. It was a traditional good-luck message, but it sounded as if she *really* meant for Frankie to break her leg. A last-minute panic knifed through her. Was this what she really wanted? To compete in a sport that made her stomach behave like a thousand frogs were break-dancing inside it? Resolutely, she ignored the feeling – and Scarlett – and made her way via the kiss-and-cry area to the edge of the rink to await her fate.

"Frankie Wills," said the commentator.

Frankie froze. That was *her* name. She tried to calm the rising tide of fear that threatened to overcome her. No! *She wasn't ready.* Her feet felt like they were cast in concrete. She wouldn't be able to skate, never mind jump. *Help!*

"Frankie Wills?" A man in a blue tracksuit tapped her politely on the shoulder.

It was no good. She couldn't get out of it now. Frankie stepped onto the ice to hearty applause, most of which seemed to be coming from her family on the far side of the rink. Oh, heavens... Was her brother *whooping*? She grinned to herself and, feeling better now, she struck a pose – hands on hips, head and shoulders back – and waited.

When it came, the very first note of Ravel's "Bolero" wiped all doubt from her mind. Smiling happily, she felt like she *belonged* on the ice. Suddenly bursting with confidence, Frankie pushed off, straight into the pull-up spin, her skate gliding effortlessly across the ice…next, the stag jump, her knee bent beneath her, arms outstretched, landing softly…and twirling gracefully into the layback spin… She slowed, gathering herself for the flying camel at the heart of her routine.

And then it happened.

Her right skate jolted as it landed on the ice and, in sickening slow motion, slid away from her until – THWACK – she came down to earth, her right shoulder bouncing painfully on the hard surface.

The music went on without her.

In stunned disbelief, Frankie looked up. This wasn't supposed to happen. It *couldn't* happen. Gripped by a determination more powerful than any feeling she'd ever known, she sprang to her feet and swooshed away. Though she'd only been down for a couple of seconds, she'd missed her window for the sit spin. Knowing that it was better to go with the music rather than try to fudge it, she added extra crossovers into her routine to fill the gap. And a double Lutz for good measure. It couldn't do any harm. She'd fallen, hadn't she? It was now up to Frankie to show the judges that her routine was dazzling enough to eclipse the terrible mistake.

She knew what she had to do.

As she sped towards the final combination of jumps, she was seized with a fierce determination. And then she went for it. First, she sprang like a gazelle into the double Salchow, her arm and leg swinging around, her rotation flawless. *Dink!* This time, she landed perfectly and went straight into the next jump. The all-important jump.

Frankie shot upwards, gaining more height than ever before. She spun round once…twice…*three times*…and landed, without a wobble. Swooshing swiftly into the final spin, she lifted her arms high and watched the world go out of focus.

It was over.

She'd done a triple toe-loop. Three wonderful revolutions of pure magic. It didn't matter that it was forbidden by Madame. After the terrible fall, it was the only way she could claw her way back into the competition.

The crowd hollered their approval. It seemed

they'd already forgotten her impromptu collision with the ice. Frankie curtsied, wincing as pain shot through her shoulder. *Ouch!* That hurt. But there was no time to think about it now. Remembering to keep smiling, she stroked smoothly towards the barrier, where the coaching director waited. Her expression was impossible to read.

Suddenly, the enormity of what she'd done hit Frankie. She'd disobeyed Madame Kristiana von Berne and was now in serious danger of being thrown out of the Ice Palace. And what good would success at the British Junior Championships do her if her Olympic dream lay in tatters?

Frankie gulped. "Sorry—"

"You did the triple," said Madame von Berne, her eyes boring into Frankie's. "Go and wait for me in the hall. Now."

That was it, then. It didn't matter if Frankie did well in the competition. She'd blown it. Numb with disappointment, she ignored the door that led to the changing room and made her way out of the ice rink and into the foyer. She was going to miss hearing her results. But it no longer mattered what marks she was given. She'd just announced her retirement.

Frankie sat down hard on the wooden bench outside. Then, emotion getting the better of her at last, she burst into loud, noisy tears.

"Frankie?"

She had no idea how long she'd been sitting there. Her tears had dried, but the horror at her expulsion from the Ice Palace was brand new. Slowly, Frankie looked up at the coaching director. Her mouth became horribly dry and she swallowed with difficulty. "Yes?" she croaked.

"A word, please?" said Madame von Berne.

Frankie nodded. Did she need to ask permission? Apart from the two of them, the corridor was deserted.

Madame von Berne got straight to the point. "Would you like to explain yourself?"

Frankie didn't see why, not when she was going to be sent home anyway, but she did her best to put her scrambled thoughts into words. "The thing is…I so desperately wanted to do it," she began. "I knew that you didn't want me to and I'd decided to stick with the double toe-loop. But when I fell, I knew it was the only way to stand a chance of winning. I *had* to go for the triple. So I did it. And I'm so, so sorry for disobeying you, but…but… well, it was the only logical thing to do and I did it." She took a quick breath before she passed out from lack of oxygen.

"I see," said Madame, her voice wobbling. She sounded *really* angry.

Figuring that she had to look up soon or she'd get a crick in her neck, Frankie sneaked a peek at the coach. To her surprise, Madame von Berne was dabbing at her eye with a perfectly ironed handkerchief. Was she *crying*? Oh dear, this wasn't the reaction she'd expected at all. She wasn't sure she could deal with anyone else's tears.

"I'm sorry," said the coach shakily. Then she did the last thing in the world that Frankie expected. She laughed.

Frankie stared, utterly gobsmacked by the coach's reaction. So that hadn't been a tear of sadness she'd seen Madame wiping away. It was a tear of laughter!

"You remind me so much of myself," said the coach. "Your love of figure skating is so *real*, so utterly *true*. Do you know," she added confidentially, even though there was no one else there, "technical brilliance can put a skater on the podium, but it's drive, determination and pure talent that wins gold." Her ice-maiden expression gave way, just briefly, to a beatific smile. "You, Frankie Wills, are a natural."

Not sure how to reply, Frankie smiled back. "Does this mean I can come back to Switzerland?" she asked.

The smile faded. "On one condition," said Madame Kristiana von Berne, coaching director for Team GB, almost-Olympic-champion and fierce taskmaster. "You never – and I mean *never* – disobey me again. This time, you showed me that you have what it takes to be a winner. Next time, your bags will be packed quicker than you can say 'triple toe-loop'. Do I make myself understood?"

"Yes," squeaked Frankie.

"Then I suggest you go to the changing room and wait with the others," said the coach. "Now, go!"

Frankie didn't need to be told twice.

CHAPTER *Twenty-Three*

By the time she got back to the changing room, the British Junior Championships were all but over. Everyone had competed. Everyone would know their marks by now, all except Frankie – she'd left the arena before the judges had decided. They were just waiting for the medal ceremony. But Frankie was so deliriously happy, she didn't really care who made it onto the podium. She still couldn't believe that after all she'd done, she would be welcomed back to the Ice Palace. She would be so good. She wouldn't put a foot wrong. Deciding to keep a low profile now that she knew she was definitely staying, she tiptoed to a quiet corner and watched events unfold.

Alesha had done well, if the cheesy grin were anything to go by.

Dylan and Milly, too. And Woody.

Flic had hobbled off the ice after taking a tumble, but the others reckoned that her injuries weren't career-threatening.

"Has anyone seen Scarlett?" asked Alesha, her voice the only thing to interrupt the happy static of Frankie's thoughts.

Woody rolled his eyes. "Didn't want to come back here to sit with the mere mortals," he said. "I expect she's hobnobbing with the judges by now. Hey, Frankie!"

She'd been spotted. Grinning bashfully, Frankie came over to join the others. Now that they'd all competed, the mood was noticeably cheerier. "So who won the girls' competition?" she asked.

"Scarlett…" sighed Alesha. "But she deserved it. Her triple Lutz was pretty near perfect, by all accounts. We'll never hear the end of it, you know. Me, I'm just thrilled that I didn't end up on the ice." Realizing what she'd said, she grimaced. "Oops… But you did really well though, didn't you? You got—"

"To be honest, I don't care how I did," Frankie interrupted quickly. "I'm staying at the Ice Palace and that's all that matters. Madame's let me off the hook. But I'll be hanged, drawn and quartered if I do it again."

Milly gasped.

"No, not *really*," Frankie said quickly, as everyone exploded into laughter.

"Would all competitors gather rinkside?" drawled the woman over the loudspeaker.

"Come on," said Frankie. "Let's go and witness Scarlett's moment of glory." No matter how mean the girl had been to her, she didn't have the heart to begrudge her extra cheers.

"Stop gabbing and get a move on, Wills," said Dylan, with a wink.

* * *

The noise in the ice rink was deafening. It took the announcer three attempts to command enough quiet to be heard. And even then, the Wills party was noticeably unruly, wriggling about in their seats as if they were having the greatest difficulty sitting still. Frankie would have words with them later. Even stuck-up Scarlett deserved a bit of respect.

The boys' results were announced first.

John Joseph Harrison, the star of Whitley Bay Ice Rink, got the bronze. Silver went to Woody, whose already rosy cheeks glowed even brighter as he accepted his medal. And Frankie was delighted when Dylan was awarded gold. After his moment of glory on the podium, she congratulated him.

"Why didn't you *say?*" she asked.

"Ah, no one likes a show-off," he muttered, grinning all the same. "Hey, listen," he said, quickly changing the subject. "It's the girls' results now."

Frankie turned back to the rink, pulling her tracksuit top a little tighter and folding her arms. Even with a huge audience to warm it, the glamorous old palace was still chilly.

"With a score of 61.50," said the announcer, "the bronze medal goes to Milly Black."

"Hurray!" cried Frankie. It was a shame Milly hadn't won gold, but she'd got a medal at least. She watched as her friend shyly approached the podium. "Well done!"

"I wish they'd just get on with it," muttered Scarlett, who'd rejoined them all. She looked impatient and just a little cross. Then, spotting Frankie, she laughed shortly. "Man, are *you* in trouble! First, you headbutt the ice. Then you perform a move that Madame expressly forbade you to do." She waggled her finger and tutted annoyingly. "Naughty, naughty."

Frankie rolled her eyes.

"And," said the announcer, "with 63.00 points, the silver goes to Frankie Wills."

"Huh?" Frankie didn't understand. Had she heard right? Did her ears need syringing? She couldn't possibly have won silver, could she? *Could she?* It was only when the others began thumping her on the back that she realized it was true. No wonder her family had been restless. Was that what

Alesha had been trying to tell her? Was that why Dylan had looked so pleased? She'd come second!

Her mouth an O of utter astonishment, Frankie tried to speak, but couldn't. Luckily, the crowd did it for her. They hollered and cheered, as if she'd won. And it wasn't just the tiny Wills support team on the far side of the rink. *Everyone* was joining in.

It had to be the best feeling ever.

Slithering onto the ice like a beginner, she eventually reached the podium and wavered unsteadily on the second tier as the beautiful and very shiny medal was hung around her neck. Frankie gazed happily around the audience, thinking that this had to be the happiest moment of her life so far. She was doing what she loved best. She was lucky enough to be returning to the Ice Palace to continue living the dream. And – silently, she apologized again to Madame von Berne – she'd performed a triple toe-loop. Out of the corner of her eye, she saw Scarlett impatiently waiting for her moment of glory, but for now, everyone was cheering her.

Frankie's first couple of months at the Ice Palace

lay behind her now. She'd been transformed from a gawky beginner to a silver medallist. Now there were just a few weeks until the Christmas holidays – and then what? More training sessions, more practice, more amazing skating… And beyond that, a future so glittering that it made her eyes water.

Gently, she touched the medal that hung heavily around her neck and ran her fingers over its cold surface. She smiled. This time, it was silver, but Frankie Wills would make sure that her next medal was gold.

DON'T MISS WHAT HAPPENS NEXT, IN FRANKIE'S
SECOND TERM AT *Skate School*...

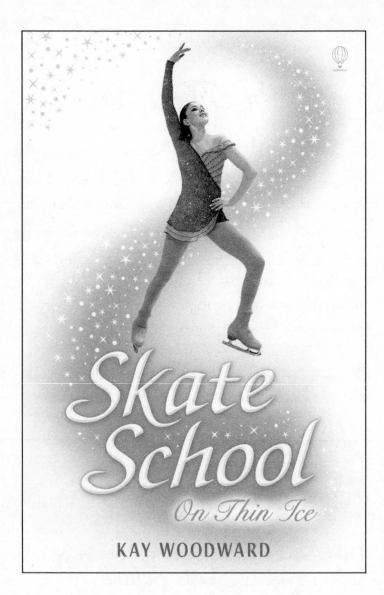

Skate
School
On Thin Ice

KAY WOODWARD

On Thin Ice

Frankie's thrilled when she's chosen to skate with Paul in a high-profile competition. He's a good friend and brilliant on the ice. But Paul wants to skate alone. He wants to keep the spotlight – and the chance to win gold – to himself. It's a real problem when they're meant to be competing in Perfect Pairs. Together!

ISBN 9780746099261

And check out

www.skate-school.net

for more Skate School gossip!

If you like Skate School, you'll love...

School Friends

Secrets, hopes, dreams...
These girls share more than just a dorm!

First Term at Silver Spires
ISBN 9780746072240
Katy's nervous about going to boarding school for the first time – especially with the big secret she has to hide.

Drama at Silver Spires
ISBN 9780746072257
Georgie's desperate to get her favourite part in the school play, but she's up against some stiff competition.

Rivalry at Silver Spires
ISBN 9780746072264
Grace is eager to win in the swimming gala for Hazeldean – until someone starts sending mean messages about her.

Princess at Silver Spires
ISBN 9780746089576
Naomi hates being the centre of attention, but when she's asked to model for a charity fashion show, she can't say no.

Secrets at Silver Spires
ISBN 9780746089583
Jess is struggling with her schoolwork and has to have special classes, but she can't bear to tell her friends the truth.

Star of Silver Spires
ISBN 9780746089590

Mia longs to enter a song she's written in the Silver Spires Star contest, but she's far too scared to perform onstage.

Party at Silver Spires
ISBN 9780746098646

Nicole's determined to keep her scholarship a secret, in case it stops her from making friends with her dorm.

Dancer at Silver Spires
ISBN 9780746098653

Izzy's trying to put her hopes of becoming a ballerina behind her – until the school puts on a dance show.

Dreams at Silver Spires
ISBN 9780746098660

Emily dreams of starting a cool club at school...but first she must persuade the teachers she's got what it takes.

Magic at Silver Spires
ISBN 9780746098677

Antonia and her friends must prove to her parents that she belongs at Silver Spires...before they take her back to Italy!

Success at Silver Spires
ISBN 9780746098684

Sasha is delighted when she discovers her natural talent for sports, but she faces tough competition from a rival.

Mystery at Silver Spires
ISBN 9780746098691

Bryony keeps hearing spooky noises in the night. Is the school haunted, or has the dorm got an unexpected guest?

For more sparkling reads,
check out
www.fiction.usborne.com